BEFORE
her

ENTWINED IN YOU BOOK FOUR
ASHLEE ROSE

BEFORE HER
Copyright © 2019 Ashlee Rose

First Edition

The author has asserted their moral right under the
Copyright, Designs and Patents Act, 1988, to be identified
as the author of this work.

This is a work of fiction. Names, characters, businesses,
places, events and incidents are either the products of the
authors imagination or used in a fictitious manner.
Any resemblance to actual persons, living or dead, or
actual events is purely coincidental.

Emma, Anna & Emma,
Thank you for being my number ones.
This is for you X

OTHER BOOKS BY ASHLEE ROSE

ENTWINED IN YOU SERIES:

Something New

Something To Lose

Something Everlasting

Before Her

All available on Amazon Kindle Unlimited

Only suitable for 18+ due to nature of the books.

CHAPTER ONE

I dumped my bag outside the door of my dorm and let out a massive sigh, three years in fucking university to study something I'm not even interested in.

"Carter, give it a chance," my dad said abruptly as if he could read my mind. "Enjoy it, you're eighteen. Make some friends, do what young boys do and work hard. This is all for the bigger picture, remember that." He smiled as he slapped me on the back which made me cough.

I opened the door to the stuffy room and looked at the bare walls and small bed on the right hand side of the room. I walked in and looked over at my dorm mates' side. His bed was all made up, posters of half-naked girls sitting on car bonnets stared back at me. I smirked when I saw the look on my mum's face. I threw my bag on the bed before sitting next to it.

"If you need anything at all sweetie, let me know. We are only forty minutes away," my mum mumbled as she walked over to me, kissing the top of my head then pushing my mousy brown fringe away from my eyes. "We really aren't that far from Cambridge, Carter, if you get home sick just call me." She nodded as she stepped back. "Do you need help unpacking?" she asked with glazed over eyes.

I shook my head and smiled at her. "No thanks, Mum, I'll be okay. You two better be off, don't want you getting stuck in rush hour traffic," I said bitterly as I looked at my dad who was engrossed on his blackberry.

My mum just nodded in silence as she walked towards my dad. "Time to go, Lewis." She didn't look at him, just walked out the dorm. My dad made a grunt and followed her, shutting the door behind him. I let out my breath as I flopped down on the hard mattress.

"I fucking hate England," I muttered to myself as I stared at the bare ceiling. I lifted my head off the shitty mattress and looked over at the door as the handle went. I saw this lanky, skinny blonde haired lad with piercing blue eyes with his tongue down some poor Sheila's throat. To be honest, she was pretty fucking hot from what I could see

"Oh, hey man!" he said as he noticed me gawking at him "I'm Louis, you must be my dorm roomie! What's your name?" he asked as he walked over and shook my hand excitedly

"Err, hey" I said as I sat myself up. "Carter," I mumbled at him.

"That's a thick accent you've got there, where you from?" he asked as he sat down next to me, the poor girl just looked lost while running her fingers through her hair

"Australia mate. Moved here a few weeks ago, and now I'm here in Cambridge, hating your shitty weather." I smirked at him

"It's not that bad here, honestly. I enjoy it." He took his eyes away from me and winked at the young girl who turned crimson in front of us. "What you studying?" he asked inquisitively.

"Business and English Literature," I said as I stood up and unzipped my bag. "You?"

"Same mate, we can be study buddies," he said as he patted me on the back. "Anyway, I'll leave you too it, we are heading down to the student bar tonight, always do on a Friday if you fancy it? Meet some of my mates, be good for you to get out, Aussie." He smirked.

"Yea, I might do, what time?" I asked, not really wanting to go, but it's better than sitting in this dive of a room.

"About eight, mate, see you down there hopefully," he said as he walked towards the young girl and pulled her out the door before closing it behind him. I suppose it wouldn't hurt going down there, might find myself a nice bit of slice to bring home.

I start to unpack and hang my bits up. I call my mum to let her know that I'm okay and that I've met my roommate. She spends half hour telling me how my dad is ignoring her, she feels like she doesn't exist to him. I sigh. I hate not being there for her, she offloads to me more than Ava. I don't mind, it just makes me feel a bit awkward when it's between her and my dad.

My dad can be an arsehole, and he has got so much worse over the last few years. I can already feel it is only going to get worse now that we are here. He has brought us over here as he has taken over a couple of struggling businesses. He has taken us away from all of our friends and family. He didn't even consider our feelings, he didn't even ask if we would be okay moving here. He is a selfish prick.

I promised myself I would stay here for the three years and then I'm fucking back off to Adelaide. I'm not staying in this shithole for no one. I was pulled back from my thoughts when my mum called out to me three times to ask if I was okay.

"Yea, sorry, Mum, just got a bit distracted in thought. I'll come and see you next weekend, okay?"

"Okay, darling," she said and I could hear the smile in her voice.

"Love you, Mum."

"Love you too," she said before hanging up the phone.

I grabbed my wash bag and towel and headed for the shower. I had no idea if Louis was coming back or whether he was balls deep in that little sort. My cock twitched at the thought of her, something about her looked so innocent. Her dark hair was shoulder length, her deep hazel eyes were big, her lips were naturally pouted and all I could think about was biting them hard while fucking her senseless.

I shook away the thoughts as the warm water hit my tanned skin. I got myself dry and pulled a grey T-shirt over my head and put a pair of skinny jeans on with my trainers. I run some hair gel through my hair and messed it up. My sage eyes looked back at me, they were dull and lifeless since being here. I missed the Australian sun, I missed the sea, I missed my friends; I was homesick.

I sprayed my cologne, then grabbed my keys and phone on the way out of my dorm. It was already seven-forty-five. I was starving. After a while of wandering around and finally giving in and asking for directions I found the student bar. It was a fucking dive. It was dark and dingy and smelt like rotting feet. I heaved as the smell hit me, as I looked around for that lanky streak of piss, Louis.

I am lucky that I am broad and muscular. I smirked when I saw him, and the fit bird he was with earlier. She was wearing a short black mini skirt and a white crop top which her boobs were spilling out of. My eyes drawled up and down her, her tiny waist on show as well as her long legs. I instantly felt hard. I needed to either fuck her, or fuck someone else.

I walked up to Louis and patted him on the shoulder. "Alright, mate," I said over the shitty music.

"Carter man, you made it!" he said smiling, taking his eyes off his lady for a second.

"Are you going to introduce me?" I asked and nodded

towards her.

"Ah yea, shit man. This is Rylie," he said as he looked over at her and pulled her beside him, wrapping his free arm round her tiny waist. "Rylie, this is Carter." He smiled at her before looking back at me.

"Nice to meet you, Rylie." I smiled at her.

"Ditto." She smiled at me, her eyes looking me up and down. "Want a drink, mate? You Aussies drink Fosters, don't ya?" he asked as he signalled the bar tender.

"Nah mate, we don't. That shit is poison. I'll have a vodka and coke," I replied as Louis nodded and faced the bartender.

"Chris, two vodka cokes and a glass of white for Rylie," he said before handing him over the cash. Minutes later he shoved the plastic cup in my hand.

"Thanks mate," I said as I took a sip. The cheap vodka burned my throat, and not in a good way. It was rancid.

"No problem, just going for a slash. Be back in five," Louis said before walking over to the toilets. I stood just staring at Rylie. I couldn't get images of her stark bollock naked out of my head.

"So, how you finding it here?" she asked me as she stepped closer, the smell of her perfume swept through my nostrils.

"Not bad, I suppose it isn't that bad." I smiled at her. "So, how long have you and Louis been together?" I asked as I took another sip of my drink.

"Oh, we aren't together. We just sleep together, but we aren't exclusive. If he fancies someone else, then he goes and does what he wants," she said as she fluttered her long lashes while taking a sip of her wine. "And vice versa." She continued as she pulled her cup away from her lips. I was mesmerized by her, I could just stare at her and let the dirty thoughts fly around my head.

"I'm back, Aussie," Louis said as he squeezed my shoulders. "What you been talking about?" he asked as he took his drink off the bar.

"Oh, not a lot," I said. "Just asked Rylie how long you two have been a thing," I said, hinting that he tells me his side of this arrangement.

"We aren't a couple, mate," he said laughing. "We just fuck." He nodded while smiling proud, and I watched as Rylie elbowed him in the ribs before blushing.

"Oh right, nice arrangement," I muttered.

"I'm going to see my mates, see you in a bit," she said to Louis as she walked towards me. "See you around, Carter."

My breath caught as my name slipped off of her tongue like silk. Fuck. I needed her.

I watched over my shoulder as her hips swayed side to side as she headed towards a big crowd of girls. I watched as her eyes met mine, followed by her group of friends. Yea they were hot, but not like her. Fuck she was sexy.

"Like what you see then, mate?" Louis interrupted me.

"Yea, I do." I sighed as I faced him.

"Mate, if you want her, you can have her. I have a few girls lined up anyway," he said, boasting.

"What?" I said laughing at his comment.

"I have a few, I don't settle down, mate. Just fuck the ones I want, when I'm bored I move on, then I move back if I fancy it again. Rylie is just too good to give up though, but I don't mind if you wanna spend a night with her," he said coolly as he sipped from his cup.

"You're fucking mental." I laughed out loud at him.

"Mate, trust me. Best way to be. No needy girls, no worrying about a wandering eye. It's just sex, and fucking hot sex at that," he said. "Anyway, come on, let me introduce you to my friends," he said as he walked past me. I rolled my eyes at him and followed him into the crowds.

I couldn't stop thinking about Rylie. He has given me the go ahead, so that's it. I am going to graft on her, then take her back to her room and make her realise that being with me is so much better than what she has with Louis.

CHAPTER TWO

After spending about half an hour with Louis and his mates, I decided I had had enough. I said my goodbyes and made my way back to my dorm. I felt beat. I hadn't seen Rylie anymore that night which disappointed me, but she will find me if she wants me.

I bit my lip and smirked as I got myself undressed down to my boxers. I got into my shitty bed and put my phone on charge. It wasn't even late, but my eyes were getting heavy before giving in to sleep.

I jumped when I heard the dorm door slam. I sat up, heart racing. It took me a moment to realise I wasn't at home.

Before I could lean over and switch the lamp on I felt someone lean onto my bed. My eyes adjusted to the dark when I saw her. Rylie. Fuck.

"Everything––" I was interrupted when I felt her plump lips on mine. I could taste the shitty wine on her breath, but I wasn't complaining.

Her tongue entered my mouth harshly as she caressed it on every stroke. I thrusted my hands into her hair and tugged on it gently which released a slight moan from her lips as she slid herself onto my lap.

I could feel myself harden underneath her. I let go of her hair and pushed her skirt around her waist. I pulled away and took in the view of her. She had the tiniest G-string on. I bit my lip as I took a deep breath in through my teeth.

"You sure you want to do this?" I asked.

"Never been surer." She smiled at me, her hazel eyes glistening. I crashed my lips back onto hers as I pulled her knickers to the side and slid two fingers easily into her soaking opening.

I watched as she moaned, throwing her head back as she started riding my fingers. I brushed my thumb against her clit which made her cry out and buck her hips forward as I pushed my fingers into her deeper.

"Fuck me," she whispered. "Now."

Her eyes were dark and hazy as she intoxicated me with her look. How could she be the same shy girl I met earlier that day? I didn't mutter a word. I pulled my bed sheet that was between us away and pushed my boxers down to my ankles.

I reached across to my bedside unit, switching the lamp on, then pulled out a condom and rolled it down as quick as I could. I was throbbing for her. I lifted her tiny frame up as I slid my thick, long cock inside her. I watched her mouth move from an 'o' to a satisfied smile. She was so tight. I continued to thrust myself hard and fast into her, watching her boobs move with her hips movements was turning me on more than I already was.

"Carter," she moaned out. "Oh, fuck, Carter," she cried.

I smirked as I watched me undo her. I felt her tight muscles clamp round me as her climax was getting close. I hate having sex with a condom but needs must.

I felt myself building, sat myself up and pulled her top down so her breasts were free before putting one of them into my mouth and sucking hard. That's all it took. She screamed out my name as she came, hard. I followed her as I thrust into her a few more times before burying my head into her neck.

We sat in silence as we both came down from our highs. I sat back against the headboard and marvelled at her.

"What are you staring at?" she said shyly.

"You," I said bluntly.

"Well, I must admit, Carter, you fuck good," she said as she went to move off me.

I grabbed her hips and held her still. "Not yet, just stay with me for a minute," I said quietly.

"You sure? I don't mind just going," she said nervously.

"I don't want you to just go," I said quietly.

"Okay, I'll stay." She smiled. "Just for a minute."

I pulled her down to me and kissed her again. I'm not sure if she felt it, but I definitely felt something for her.

"Let me go freshen up, you got a tee I can wear, hunk?" she asked.

"Of course, babe, in the wardrobe." I smiled at her. She threw me a wink before hopping off me. I watched as she walked away. Damn. She is fucking hot.

I got rid of my condom and pulled my boxers back up. Within minutes she was fresh faced and wearing just my T-shirt. I could feel myself harden again. How can I be ready to go already?! I shook my head as she sauntered over to me.

"Why you shaking your head?" she asked as she wrapped her hair around her finger.

"I'm shaking it at you." I smirked

"Why?"

"'Cos, you were amazing, plus you look hot," I mumbled.

"You don't look too bad yourself." She winked "What's your last name?"

"Cole." I winked back at her.

"Well, Cole, is there any room in that tiny bed for me?" she asked playfully

"Of course, come slide in next to me." I groaned as she slipped in and lay in front of me. My heart raced as my skin touched hers, there was no denying there wasn't a spark that tingled through me. I wrapped my arms over her pulling her towards me and breathed her scent in.

"Night, Rylie."

"Night, Cole."

I rolled and woke to see Rylie no longer next to me. I pulled myself out of bed, entered the bathroom and jumped under the shower. I wrapped my towel around me and sat back on my bed when I saw the door open. A smile crept across my face when I saw Rylie walk in. She was still wearing my T-shirt, but it was tucked into her black mini.

"Morning, Cole." She smiled at me. "Hungry?" she asked as she sat on the bed next to me and placed a kiss on my cheek.

"Famished." I smiled back at her. "What you bought me?" I asked, teasingly.

"Coffee and croissants," she said quietly.

"Perfect." I beamed at her as I took the hot coffee off of her. "This is the first time I've had breakfast in bed."

"Me too," she mumbled as she took a sip of her coffee. Our breakfast was interrupted when I heard the dorm door open.

"Oh, morning, Aussie, Rylie." Louis winked as he walked through the door. "Good night?" He eyed us both up.

"Yea, mate," I said, feeling agitated.

"Good. Rylie what you doing later?" he asked her.

"Probably spend it with Carter, haven't got any plans."

I couldn't help the smile that spread across my face.

"What about you?" she asked.

"Going to sleep, then probably head out with the lads," he said then nodded his head at me before disappearing into the bathroom.

"Awkward," she whispered.

"Mmm", I mumbled. "Anyway, forget about that. I would love to spend the day with you, if you haven't changed your mind." I took a bite of the buttery croissant.

"Of course I haven't, but I wanna go home and get showered. Then I'll be back." She giggled.

I watched as she got off the bed and made her way to the door. "See you in a bit, Cole." She blew me a kiss and disappeared out the door.

I sat and twiddled my thumbs while I tried to think of something I could do with Ryley today when I saw Louis appear.

"So, good night, mate?" I asked.

"Yea, Aussie. Banged a hottie. Standard." he winked "I would ask how yours went but I can guess." He chuckled as he slipped into his bed.

"Yea, it was good, mate. She is out of this world," I said as I looked towards the window. "But look, if it's too weird then let me know. You know, bro code and all that. Do you have that here? Or is it just an Aussie thing?" I asked nervously, not sure why I was nervous.

"Nah, mate, it's fine. Yea, we do have bro code, but you ain't breaking it. I gave you the go ahead. Just watch that one, she isn't as innocent as she seems. And don't come crying when she comes back to me." He chuckled out loud. I laughed along with him.

"No fucking chance," I whispered to myself.

"Anyway, night, fucker. See you later. There is a party in the main house on campus if you wanna come later? Lots of new snatch there." He laughed and rolled over.

I will be going tonight, but I won't be looking for any new 'snatch' as he put it. I walked towards the wardrobe and pulled out jeans and a jumper and put my cap on my messy hair. I then text my mum to let her know I was okay while I waited for Rylie. Let's just hope she doesn't stand me up.

What the fuck is wrong with me, I have never been like this about a girl.

Man up, Cole. She's just a fuck... isn't she?

CHAPTER THREE

After about twenty-minutes Rylie showed up. I opened the door to her, looking her up and down in her tight skinny jeans and low cut vest top.

"Hey," I muttered to her as I closed the door behind me.

"Hey, handsome," she said quietly.

"What do you fancy doing?" I asked her.

"I'm easy, lunch and a get to know you chat." She smiled.

"Sounds great," I replied, nodding at her. I walked beside her in idle chit chat until we came to a little bistro on campus. It looked okay from the outside, I was a bit of a food snob. We were shown to our table by the waitress on the door, and I ushered Rylie forward as I followed close behind her. I watched as she smiled and thanked the waitress and passed me a menu

"You're not one of these girls that orders a salad and pushes it around your plate, are you?" I asked, raising my brow with a sarcastic smile on my face.

"No I'm bloody not, I love my food." She giggled as she eyed up the menu. "What about you? Are you fussy?" she questioned as she peered at me over the top of her menu.

"Nah, I'm not fussy. I eat most things to be honest." I smiled back at her then gave her a cheeky wink.

The waitress came back quickly and asked for our order. I gestured for Rylie to order first as she tucked her hair behind her ear.

"I will have the double extreme cheeseburger and strawberry milkshake please," she said with her eyes glistening.

The waitress noted her order then faced me. "That sounds good, I will have the same but with a chocolate milkshake instead."

I closed the menu and took Rylie's off of her before passing it back to the waitress. "Cheers," I muttered as she walked away from us.

"Where the hell do you put all your food?" I asked, confused.

"Oh, I don't worry about that, I work it off anyway," she said teasingly. It instantly made me jealous. I knew she was talking about fucking around with other guys, but I didn't want her fucking around with anyone but me.

"How about you just worry about working it off with me?" I said boldly, keeping my sage eyes on her big, hazel ones.

"Easy, tiger, I'm not looking for anything serious," she said with a stammer, breaking eye contact. "Not yet anyway."

My heart stopped as she flicked her eyes back up to mine.

"I didn't say anything about being 'serious,'" I said, air quoting the *serious* bit. "I just don't want you fucking anyone else but me." my mouth twitched. "Would that work for you?" I asked. My heart was thumping, waiting for her response.

"Well, I don't see why not." She smiled at me.

"Well, that's good." I let out a sigh as I saw the waitress appear with our milkshakes.

After watching her demolish the monster burger that we had both ordered, I decided to get to know her a bit better. "So, what are you studying?" I asked.

"English literature and English history," she said as she finished her milkshake. I nodded, impressed.

"Well, at least I get to see you in English literature," I said as I mixed the bottom of the milkshake with my straw. "Do you like it here?" I asked.

"It's not bad, it wasn't my first choice but I'm glad I got in here," she said, nodding to herself. "You glad you moved over here?" she asked inquisitively.

"Not really," I scoffed "I liked living back in Australia. Just had to follow my dad unfortunately." I shook my head.

"But, I am glad I am here because I met you, and Louis." I chuckled. "Can't forget about that lanky streak of piss," I said smirking and watching her reaction.

"Are all Australian's as good looking as you?" she asked boldly.

"Ha, no, babe. I am one of a kind." I flashed her my pearly whites with a massive grin

"Well, I got lucky then," she teased. I signalled for the waitress to come over, so I could pay our bill.

Once paid, I took Rylie's hand and led her out of the bistro. There were a group of lads standing outside. I held her hand tight as we started our walk past them. I was okay, but I could tell she wasn't.

As we approached them, a tall, black haired boy shouted at her. "Hey, Rylie, fancy coming over and giving me some loving tonight? My cock is throbbing, and I know you love a good cock, you dirty bitch."

His little group all laughed at his degrading comment. I felt my temper rising.

"Carter, please, don't react to him. He is a nobody," she begged as she tugged on my arm, pulling me in the other direction.

"Come on, baby, don't leave me waiting. You know you want to be bouncing up and down on my dick." He sniggered. That was it. I dropped her hand and ran over to him. Not thinking about the consequences I threw a punch into his nose, knocking him to the floor. I didn't stop. His nose had exploded by this point, but I continued to punch him before grabbing him by the front of his T-shirt as I lifted him slightly off the floor and smashed him back down again.

"Apologise," I said through gritted teeth.

"She's a slut. She doesn't deserve an apology." he smirked, his teeth covered in blood.

I lifted him back up again and head-butted him as he fell to the floor holding his nose.

"I said apologise," I said with a raised voice. I heard the scamper of feet behind me as his friends left him at my clutches.

"Fine! Fine! Rylie, I'm sorry!" he shouted.

"Pathetic piece of shit, mate," I said spitting at him. Before I could lift myself off of him I felt hands on me pulling me away.

"Get off me," I shouted as I noticed I was being pulled away by campus security. Shit.

I looked at Rylie who had her hands over her mouth as she watched me being dragged away. I looked over my shoulder to see the piece of shit being helped to his feet and walked away by more security. I am such a dick, I had to let my temper get in the way. I should have listened to Rylie and left it. I am in such deep shit. My dad is going to kill me.

I bowed my head in defeat and walked into the main building.

Fuck knows what was going to happen now.

ASHLEE ROSE

I sat in front of Master Tyrell in his impressive office, feeling belittled as soon as I walked in.

"Mr Cole," he said with a disappointing tone in his voice. His greying black hair was slicked back, his green eyes tired and worn. "You have not even been here a full two days and you have got yourself in trouble," he said, shaking his head.

"But, sir," I started, before he held is hand up, silencing me.

"I don't care what your excuse is. I currently have a student with two black eyes and a broken nose because of you. How do you think that looks on me? What am I going to tell his parents?" he asked.

"I'm sorry, sir," I said, like the naughty school kid I was.

"If it wasn't for your father's generous donation to our struggling funds, I would have no choice but to expel you," he said as he rested his chin on his two index fingers, his elbows resting on the desk. "One last chance, Cole. No fucking up. How about putting some of that anger into a physical activity?" he suggested.

The only physical activity I could think of was Rylie.

"Maybe boxing? Or American football? Something to channel your anger on," he said brightly. I just nodded. "I mean it, Cole. One last chance. Now get out," he said sternly. I nodded keeping my mouth shut as I left the office. I closed the door behind me to see Louis and Rylie waiting outside

27

his office for me.

"How much shit did you get in, Aussie?" Louis asked. I shrugged him off and made my way to Rylie. Her eyes black where her makeup had smudged.

"You okay?" I asked as I brushed my thumb across her cheek.

"I'm fine, especially now I know you are okay." She sniffed.

"I'm okay," I said as I pulled her into an embrace, kissing the top of her head.

"Thank you," she mumbled into my chest.

"No problem, babe," I replied.

After a few minutes Louis patted me on the back and hugged Rylie. I shook my head at the last hour or so as we made our way back to our dorm. I needed a few hours to chill out. I said goodbye to Rylie as we dropped her at her dorm.

"See you tonight, yea?" I asked her, searching her beautiful eyes.

"Maybe. I don't feel up to anything at the moment. Just want a hot shower," she said, her voice small.

"Don't let that prick ruin it. He won't say nothing again, and neither will anyone else," I snapped.

"I'll see. Bye, Carter," she mumbled as she closed the door on me. I stepped back and took a deep breath.

"Have I fucked it up?" I turned round to Louis, confused.

"I dunno, Aussie, she does seem pissed. Maybe she is just embarrassed. Give her a few hours. Don't stew on it. Plenty of other girls there tonight," he said as we started walking towards our dorm.

"I don't want any other girl. Don't you get that? I ain't you, mate. With your little arrangement with fucking and chucking," I said angrily. I felt my brow furrow as I stared at him, "I ain't in the mood, mate, so don't push me," I snapped barging pass him.

"Chill out, mate." He laughed. "Think you are whipped, Aus," he said, making a whipping noise behind me.

"Fuck off, Louis," I said bluntly before flipping him off with my middle finger. "Go swivel you jerk." I heard him laugh at me, but I wasn't biting anymore. It wasn't him I was really pissed at. I was pissed at myself.

I only have myself to blame for fucking it up with Rylie. I'm such a prick. I got to the dorm before Louis and slammed the door behind me, then headed to the shower. I needed a cool shower. I needed to calm down, dampen my anger. I was letting everything rile up in me, and that wasn't good. I needed to speak to my mum. No doubt they have been called anyway, but I need her to calm me down. She is the only one who can shake me from this shit mood I'm in.

I groaned as I stepped into the shower. I ain't ready to give Rylie up yet, and I'm not going to let today ruin what we have had. Yea, it's been two days, but I am already falling for her. This girl has a hold of me, and I can't just forget about her. I heard Louis muttering something into the bathroom.

"Fuck off, Louis!" I shouted. I rolled my eyes when I heard him enter the bathroom

"Louis!" I shouted as I stuck my head round the curtain. "Fuck off," I seethed at him, but it wasn't till I saw her, it was Rylie.

"Shit, Rylie. Sorry. I thought you were Louis," I said ashamed. She didn't say anything, just stripped down to her gorgeous skin before hopping in the shower, wrapping her tiny arms around me and placing her hands on my chest. Her frame pushed up behind me. We didn't say anything. Just stood in silence, letting the hot water wash over both of us.

We didn't need to talk, this was all we needed. Just me and her. I didn't want to move, and I didn't intend to. I felt her plush lips plant soft kisses across the back of my shoulder blades.

"I'm sorry," she mumbled against my wet skin. I turned around to face her, cupping her beautiful face in my hands.

"You don't need to apologise," I reassured her before bending my neck down and kissing her full lips hard, slipping my tongue in as I savoured this moment. Before I could think about what I said, it slipped out in a whisper on her lips.

"Be mine, only mine. Don't ever leave me Rylie."

I opened my eyes as I burned into her soul, waiting for her response. She didn't say anything but answered with a kiss, a kiss so hard and passionate no words were needed. I knew she felt the same, and that's all I wanted. Me and her.

CHAPTER FOUR

We decided to leave the party tonight, Louis was gutted but he soon got over it thinking about the girls he could be with. Rylie asked if she could spend the night, which of course I didn't decline. I loved having her in my T-shirts and snuggled into me. I pulled out my Mac and booted it up.

"What do you want to watch babe?" I asked her.

"Something easy, how about Pretty Woman?" She beamed up at me. I reacted by rolling her eyes at her

"Fine!" I sighed. "But, if you tell anyone then I will kill you," I teased before breaking into a laugh. "Anything to make you happy." I kissed the top of her head as I waited for Pretty Woman to download. I hopped up and grabbed a couple of bags of popcorn that my mum had packed into my suitcase before settling back down with her.

I watched her face as she watched the film, I loved that she got so engrossed into it. The emotions on her face were so apparent that I couldn't stop staring. It was late by the time the film finished and we were both exhausted, so I slid behind her pulling the covers over me then wrapped my arms across her and spooning behind her.

The last couple of months have flown, I was actually enjoying business studies and English lit more than I thought I would. Me and Rylie were going from strength to strength and were spending as much time as possible with each other, with the occasional third wheel we called Louis.

I was packing my bags up as I was heading home to Mum's for the weekend like I did every other weekend. It's nice getting a bit of space and different scenery from the same sights of the campus.

I was interrupted when I heard the door go and saw Rylie walk towards me in a short mini and cropped vest top.

"Hey, you," she said as she kissed me on the cheek.

"Hey," I said I continued to pack.

"I'm sorry I can't come again, I am just swamped with work for this terms exam in English history. You're not mad, are you?" she asked me quietly.

"Of course I'm not mad, I just wish you were coming with me that's all, but it's only two days. It's really not that long." I smiled a little smile at her as I zipped my holdall up.

"What time will you be back Sunday?" she asked while nibbling the skin around her nails.

"Probably about five-ish I suppose, how come?" I asked as I wrapped my arms around her, pulling her close to me. I want her, but my mum will be here any minute, so I can't risk it.

"Just so I know, baby. I can make sure I am finished with work and ready for you to take full advantage of me," she said as she bit her full bottom lip.

"Don't bite your lip," I said under my breath.

"How come?" she teased as she sunk her teeth back into it.

I grabbed her chin with my hand and pulled her towards me, letting our lips crash into each other. I couldn't stop myself, I ran my hands to her exposed thighs and pushed her skirt to her waist and yanked her delicate knickers to the side. I didn't muck about with foreplay, no need for condoms anymore as she was on the pill and we have both been tested.

I pulled away from her and led her to my bed before twisting her round and pushing her forward onto my bed, so her arse was in the air. It was a fucking fantastic sight, my dick throbbed through my jeans.

I quickly unbuckled my belt and ripped my button undone as I shoved my jeans down to my knees.

"This will be hard and fast, baby," I said, already out of breath. I listened as she panted while nodding at me. I took her hips into my hands and slid myself into her soaked sex, smiling as she whimpered then moaned as she took all of me.

I upped my pace as I smashed into her as deep as I

could. I wasn't slowing my rhythm and she started to cry out as her breathing quickened, her muscles tightening around my cock which indicated she was getting close.

"That's right, baby, come for me," I said in a low growl, punishing her with harder thrusts that I knew she loved. I bit my lip as she screamed out my name as she reached her climax, pushing me to my own high, making me moan her name as I came undone inside her.

After stilling for a moment I pulled myself out and slid her panties back across. I knelt down and planted a kiss on her arse cheek.

"As banging as ever." I smirked as I stood up and adjusted myself in my boxers before buckling my jeans up. I watched as she rolled over, licking her lips and looking at me while shimming her skirt down.

"Oh, Cole, you are good," she said, her face flustered.

"You ain't too bad yourself, sweetheart," I cooed.

"Carter, darling." I heard my mum's voice as she swung through the door. "You ready?" She looked at me, then the bed, confused. "Everything okay?" she asked, her brows heightened.

How fucking close was that?!

"Yea, fine, Mum. This is Rylie," I said, helping Rylie off the bed.

"Mrs Cole, pleasure to meet you," Rylie said as she walked towards my mum then hugging her.

"Oh." my mum squeaked, clearly surprised by her

affection. "Hello, dear, so nice to meet you. But please, call me Elsie," my mum said with her sweet smile spreading across her face.

"Thank you, Elsie. I better be off, but it was so nice to meet you." She smiled before turning to me. "See you soon, Cole." She winked before closing the door behind her.

"Oh, she seems nice, darling," my mum chirped up, staring at the closed door before focusing back on me.

"Yea, she's a good one." I smiled at her. "Anyway, you ready?" I asked.

"Ready when you are, darling," my mum replied.

I picked my bag up and opened the door for my mum, gesturing for her to leave before me as I followed swiftly behind her. I was glad to be out of here for a couple of days, but god I was going to miss Rylie.

-

I just sat down for Sunday lunch with my parents and Ava, my sister. It had been a well needed rest with lots of studying, and Mum's home-made cooking. I could smell the roast lamb, I couldn't wait to demolish dinner then head back to campus.

"So, how's campus?" Ava asked me while reading a magazine.

"Yea, it's alright, not too bad. Would still rather be back in Aus," I said with a frown.

"Me too. I fucking hate it here," she said as she rolled her eyes.

"Hopefully we can go back in a couple of years, go back to our roots." I shrugged.

"Can't see it happening. Dad's business is booming, he won't leave here," she said shaking her head. "I just don't see it." She sighed.

We stopped as soon as Dad walked into the room. "Why have you gone silent?" he asked.

"No reason, just thought dinner was being served up," I said back to him.

"It is, just waiting on your mother." He nodded as she came through with plates of food.

"Need any help mum?" I asked.

"No, dear, but thank you for offering." She smiled as she made her way back to the kitchen to fetch more plates.

A few minutes later she returned, and we all hung our heads as Dad said grace before tucking into our meal. A few words were exchanged over dinner but most of the time we sat in silence enjoying our food. I helped Ava wash up and put the plates away before running upstairs and grabbing my bag.

"I wish you didn't have to go," I heard Ava say as she walked into my room. "I hate being here on my own." She sulked. "All Mum and Dad do is argue, he is such a selfish prick to her. She deserves so much more than him. Not sure why she doesn't leave him." She shrugged as she flopped on my bed.

"I'm sorry I am leaving you to deal with this, but I had

no choice. Dad put me into this shitty college. Only good thing to come out of it is Rylie and Louis."

"So, you smitten with her then?" she asked me, propping herself up onto her elbows.

"Yea, Ava, I really am. I have fallen for her big time. I wanna head back early to surprise her. I told her I would be back about five, but If I leave soon I'll be back by three." I smiled.

"Ah, my brother, in love. Sweet, young love." She giggled.

"Wouldn't go that far," I teased.

"Hmm, we will see. Anyway, let's get you downstairs. No doubt Mum is waiting for you," she said as she pulled herself away from my bed. I picked my bag up and followed her out. I stopped when I saw my dad at the bottom of the stairs, holding the car keys. Great, forty minutes with him. I snorted.

"Ready, son?" he asked.

"Not really." I sighed as I scooped my mum up into a cuddle. "See you in a couple of weeks, Mum," I whispered to her. I put her down and hugged Ava goodbye. I walked with Dad to the car in silence, and as he pulled away he put the radio on for some back ground noise.

I was just about to put my ear phones in when my dad started up a conversation.

"So, Master Tyrell called me to tell me about your little brawl a few weeks ago. I'm not sure why he hadn't called sooner," he said, eyes focused on the road.

I turned my head to face him, studying his expressions. His mousy hair was thinning on top, his olive skin had soft wrinkles starting to form, his stubble was greying. He didn't look like my dad anymore; this business has aged him. Money had aged him.

"I am utterly disgusted with your behaviour, how fucking embarrassed do you think I was when he told me?!" he shouted at me.

"But, Dad––" I stammered.

"No, Carter! No "but dad.". How do you think it makes me look as a business man, to my clients? I have given that university a lot of money and you fucked up on your second day." He shook his head as he tightened his grip on the steering wheel.

"I'm sorry, Dad, but I was sticking up for Rylie," I defended myself.

"All of this for a girl!? You are a disgrace!" he banged his fist on the dash.

"She's just not a girl!!" I shouted back at him. "You know what it is like being in love!"

"Love!?" he laughed at me, belittling me. "No one is ever in love, you stupid boy. The only thing I love in my life is money and my business. It's my passion," he said smugly.

"What about Mum, me and Ava? Do you not love us?" I said with bile rising in my throat.

"Of course I do! I am just saying, you are never truly

'in' love. The love I have for you, Ava and your mother is expected. As if you are born with it." He stammered over his last words.

"You're a piece of shit," I spat.

Before he could respond I put my ear phones in and blasted Linkin' Park as loud as I could into my ear drums, praying that they burst then bled.

CHAPTER FIVE

I slammed the door walking away from my dad. I couldn't believe the pure shit that was coming out of his mouth. I need to tell my mum to fuck him off. I sulked through the hallways to my dorm, I was going to throw my bag down and make my way to Rylie. I need her, emotionally and physically. She is my calm.

"Hey, Aussie! You are back, did you miss me?" Louis chuckled to himself.

"Oh, yea, like a fucking hole in the head," I teased. "I will be back soon, I'm going to see Rylie. You around later? We will go to that dive bar and sink a couple of beers if you fancy?" I muttered as I sprayed myself with some cologne.

"Yea, bro, sounds good. Have fun with Rylie." He smiled.

"Cool. Have you seen much of her?" I asked.

"Nah, when I did see her she said she was sinking with studying. I know she has this crazy exam coming up this week, so I think she is trying to get as much in as possible."

He shook his head. "Craziness. Anyway, mush, go have fun. See you in a couple of hours," he said as he slipped into the bathroom.

I basically ran out the room and headed towards her block. My heart was racing, I just couldn't wait to see her.

I took a deep breath as I knocked on her door. I waited a few moments but there was no answer. I was confused. She knew I was coming back. I waited a few minutes before knocking again, still no answer. I grabbed the door handle and thought about turning it, knowing that I shouldn't, but my need to see her overruled my head. I twisted the handle and walked into her dorm.

"What the fuck?" I said in a whisper.

There was my Rylie moaning and panting while riding the lanky, pale piece of shit who's nose I broke all those months ago. Temper raged through me as I stormed across the room.

"Rylie!!!" I shouted.

She gasped, "Carter," as she pulled the shitty white sheet over her trying to cover her modesty even though I have seen it more times than I can count. "Oh my god, Carter, what are you doing here?" she asked, still sitting on top of him.

"Surprisingly, I was going to surprise you!" I spat at her. It took everything in me not to pull her off him and pummel a punch into his face once again, but heartbreak consumed me. I felt it shatter there, in front of her. My face dropped, my hands started to shake. How could she do this to me?

I couldn't stop staring at her, the image of her moaning because of him was going around and around in my head. My Rylie. I was distracted when she was stood in front of me with the sheet wrapped tight around her body.

"Why are you covering yourself? It's not like I haven't seen you naked," I said bitterly, spitting the words out of my mouth.

"Carter..." she said, her big, beautiful hazel eyes darting back and forth from mine. "Carter..."

I scoffed. "Sorry, is that all you can muster is my name? Was I that good in bed for you to only remember what you would moan out while riding me? Or is it because you don't know what to fucking say for being a cheat?" I said to her, I couldn't even scream. I was so deflated. How can you go from a complete high, to a complete low in minutes? She had broken, shattered and completely ruined me.

"I'm sorry" she said looking at her feet.

"Are you? Are you really. You know what, save it. My Dad was right, no one is ever in love." I stepped away from her and eyed the prick laying in the bed hiding himself. "Watch ya back, you mug. I'll be coming for you," I warned him.

"Love?" she stuttered. "You love me?" Her eyes glistened as the tears started to brim in her eyes.

I laughed in front of her. "I thought I *loved* you, but no. No, Rylie, I don't fucking love you. Now get back to your shag, and don't ever speak to me again," I shouted as I stormed for the door, slamming it behind me.

What the actual fuck?

I headed back to my room and grabbed my bag.

"Ohh, you staying there tonight you dirty bastard?" Louis called out from his bed.

"No I fucking ain't. I'm going home. I'm done," I shouted back at him.

"Carter, man, what has happened?" he asked as he jumped off his bed and headed towards me.

"Rylie! Fucking that bloke whose nose I broke. Walked in mid-fuck didn't I. I'm done mate," I said.

"No way! She was smitten with you!" Louis tried to defend her.

"Obviously fucking not." I shook my head "I should have listened man. Just a fuck. A little arrangement where I chose when and who I fuck. Like you. You don't get your heart shattered do you!?" I asked whilst bellowing at him.

"She broke your heart? Shit, man, I didn't realise you loved her..." he trailed off, his face looked lost. His eyes sad for me.

"Yea, well, shit happens. I'm gone. I can't stay here for shit. Call me in the week mate. I'll miss ya," I said as I threw more stuff into my bags.

"Don't go, man, please," Louis begged.

"I have to," I said as I zipped the last bits in my bag. I took my phone out my pocket and called my dad.

"Hey, come and get me. Now," I snapped before hanging the phone up. I pulled Louis in for a bro hug and walked out the door without saying another word.

I am never fucking falling in love again. I can't be that man. She has completely chewed me up and spat me back out. Carter Cole will never fall for a girl again, I will use them to my will, then chuck them away like she done me.

CHAPTER SIX

I burst through the double doors to the college and ran down the steps as quick as my legs took me. I saw my dad sitting outside waiting for me. I threw my bags on the back seat and jumped in the front slamming the door to his Mercedes shut.

"Son, what's happened?" he asked. I looked at him, I could see the worry on his face, the concern in his eyes.

"Rylie, Dad. That's what happened," I stammered but sounded blunt.

I could feel his eyes burning into the side of my head before he started the car and slowly pulled away. I don't know what made me look back, but I did, seeing Rylie standing on the steps of the college with her hands in her hair in utter shock that I was walking away. I slowly moved my eyes away and continued facing forward trying to calm my breathing and my thumping heart.

After what felt like hours, my dad broke the silence.

"So, do you want to talk about it?" he asked, eyes still

fixed on the road, his hands gripping tightly on the wheel.

I sighed before speaking. "I caught her fucking someone else."

"Oh," my dad said quietly. "Was it a friend?" he asked.

"No. It was the boys nose I broke when I got in trouble," I said looking down at my knuckles, watching as I clenched them as tight as I could.

"But didn't he say nasty things to her?" he muttered.

"Yup. I let my feelings get in the way. I fell in love," I said quietly. "But never again. I vow from this moment on I will never fall in love again," I said with confidence.

"Carter…" my dad replied, his voice fading off with exasperation.

"Nah, Dad, I'm taking a leaf out of your book. Don't fall in love," I said shaking my head.

"What I said before, Carter, I didn't mean it as you've taken it," he stammered.

"You meant for it sound like that, Dad. I have taken the way you wanted me to," I said bluntly. "I think you're an absolute prick for treating mum that way, but as long as she is happy, I'm happy."

"But I do love your mum," he said rubbing his chin while we were stopped at traffic lights.

"Stop bullshitting me, Dad. I don't care," I said before putting my ear phones in and losing myself in Eminem.

It wasn't long before we pulled up. I swung the door

open grabbing my bags off the back seat and storming through my front door, earphones still in. I didn't look at anyone. Just stormed upstairs slamming my bedroom door behind me. My heart hurt. I felt broken. I never wanted to feel like this again.

–

I sat at my office desk rolling the tip of my pen along my bottom lip, smirking to myself of the events that unfolded last night. Thinking back to Everly and every compromising position I had her in last night. I dropped my pen and picked up my mobile dialling her number.

"Hey, you," I purred down the phone at her.

"Hey to you too," she said quietly.

"I just thought I would give you a call to let you know that I haven't stopped thinking about you all day. We have two nights left, we are going for cocktails tomorrow, so wear something stunning. Then back to mine, so I can savour every single minute," I smiled as I heard her breath hitch.

"See you tonight, Cole," she said silkily.

"See you later," I replied before cutting her off.

–

I thought back to when this all started. When I decided to start my 'flavours' as I like to call them. After everything that happened with Rylie I decided to go back to university to finish my business degree. I kept my head down only spending time with Louis and some of his friends. I just didn't want to get caught up with anyone. Yea, I slept around but as soon as it was finished I left. The girls knew what it was about. I followed Louis' moto. Fuck them and chuck them.

I passed my business class and received a master's degree. I couldn't wait to get away from that place. Me and Louis and a few of the other guys still met up once a week, and I still continued to pick random girls up. Then I sat and thought about, why not change things up. Hire a few girls to stick to a plan and for them to be there at my beckon call. They stay with me, eat with me, do everything we want to do, then when their time is up, move onto the next one. No commitments, no feelings, no heartbreak. That's exactly what I needed.

It started off with Luna, a waitress in our local bar. She was dark haired, crystal blue eyes and drop dead gorgeous. I proposed it to her, telling her all the perks and the wage she would receive. I then started hunting around for new girls to fill up the empty spaces, and now, here I am with seven girls. Seven girls who know exactly what this arrangement is. I am never alone, and I can have my cake and eat it. Literally.

-

I couldn't believe that was nearly ten years ago. I couldn't believe I was thirty-two. I couldn't believe I was running Coles Enterprise.

I felt the lump burn in my throat as I looked at the

photo on my desk of me, Ava, Dad and Mum. That was our last photo, nearly nine years go. I hadn't long taken over the business, under my dad's watchful eye of course. The business boomed within being here for two years, so we never got to go back home.

My dad was getting worse with the more money he earned. He neglected my mum, buying her things for her happiness but all she wanted was him. The man she married and loved. But he couldn't give her that anymore. He was fully devoted to his business.

When he handed the business over to me at twenty-three, I thought he was mental. I couldn't work out why he would want an irresponsible and immature boy running his company. But it made sense. He was ill. He kept it quiet for a while, powering through, showing me the ropes and introducing me to my team of fifty that I would be in charge of. Now that number has tripled and then some.

I remember feeling so overwhelmed by it all. One evening he called me into my now office and told me to sit down. I remember having clammy hands, my heart was thumping out of my shirt, I'm sure he could see it. The words that left his lips left me crushed.

"I have cancer. I am dying. I have been given two months. Two months to make you into the best version of yourself for this company. I have made mistakes, many, many mistakes. The biggest being your mother. I never treated her how I should have, and I regret it every single

day. Don't be like me. Don't give up on love son, please."

I sat there, gobsmacked at the words that were coming out of his mouth. He didn't last two months, he didn't change his ways. He got bitter as the days went on, he didn't spend any time with us or my mum.

We fell out the day before he died. I didn't go and say goodbye, I didn't go to his bedside to be with him to tell him I forgave him. I was too stubborn and angry. That is my biggest regret. Never saying goodbye.

That only fuelled my 'flavour' situation. I couldn't get enough.

I was interrupted when I heard a knock on my door.

"Come in," I shouted.

"Mr Cole, I am sorry to interrupt but Aimee is here to see you," Erin, my assistant, muttered.

"Not a problem, let her through." I smiled and stood from my desk buttoning up my button on my charcoal grey suit jacket.

"Aimee." I smiled as I walked over and kissed her cheek. Aimee was my latest flavour, my number seven and by far my sweetest. "Everything okay?" I asked her.

"I wanted to see you, I couldn't wait another two days," she sulked.

"Well, I can't change the rota baby." I smiled at her as I pulled a chair out for her, then took my seat opposite her.

"How are you finding it? Obviously, this is your second

time on," I asked, tapping my long fingers on the desk.

"Yea, I'm enjoying it. Different." She giggled. I studied her short blonde hair, her petite frame. She really was stunning and out of all of the girls I had on, she was definitely my type.

"Good, I'm glad. And the gifts and wage, that's all okay, yes?" I asked, eyeing her the whole time.

"Yup. I can't wait to see what this week's gift is." She smiled at me.

"Is there anything you would like?" I asked.

"Well, I would LOVE a Hermes bag," she said quietly, tucking her short blonde hair behind her ears while fluttering her lashes. Oh, she was good.

"Done. Is there anything else?" I asked as I pushed myself away from my desk.

"No, thank you," she said as she stood in front of me. I grabbed her chin and tilted her head back as I took every inch of her face in. I wanted to kiss her, so bad. But, that's not how it works. I don't see two girls at the same time. I let go and walked her to the door, seeing her out.

"See you in a couple of days, Aimee."

She winked as she walked away.

Man, I wanted her now. I took a deep breath, pushing the dirty thoughts from my mind while losing myself in my work.

I couldn't wait to get home to Everly. Work took a shit

turn and I had just had enough. When I got home, dinner was sitting on the table. My stomach rumbled when I realised I hadn't eaten all day. It smelt amazing. Lamb rack on a bed of mash and greens and two glasses of red wine.

I called out to Everly but had no answer. I pulled at my tie and undone my two top buttons of my shirt when I saw her out the corner of my eye, standing stark bollock naked with a light lemon tie round her neck and her fuck me shoes.

"What you doing?" I asked, trying to hide my smile.

"I wanted to surprise you. I bought you a new tie, do you like it?" she purred running her fingers up and down it.

"It's a fucking beautiful tie." I groaned as I made my way towards her.

I slowly wrapped my fingers around the knot of the tie and pulled her softly towards me before crashing my lips into hers. Hungrily savouring every moment. I softly nipped her bottom lip before pulling away and admiring the view. Her sun kissed skin was glowing, her long blonde hair down her back. I loved her legs, they looked never ending. She was just a work of art. I wanted her. Right now.

I spun her round, moving the tie round to her back so it laid down her spine. I gave her no warning, I bent her forward over the chair, then greedily pulled my trousers and boxers down before slamming into her.

This is what I loved. I didn't have to worry about her pleasure if I didn't want to. And right now, all I cared about was mine.

I grabbed the tie and pulled it slightly. I heard her moan as she felt the slight tightening round her throat which spurred me on more. I continued my hard, punishing slams into her. I didn't care if she was uncomfortable, I needed this release.

As my climax got closer I slapped her bare arse which gave a satisfying sting, sending me to my high before I crashed down around her.

I spun her round and kissed her on the nose. "Go and get cleaned up and dressed. I'm hungry." I groaned. She nodded quietly and slipped off upstairs.

I walked around the living room of my penthouse looking at the window which looked out over the stunning city of London. I picked my glass of red up and swallowed a big mouthful, feeling satisfied as it ran down my throat like pure silk.

This is the life.

Nothing could ever change my path.

This is exactly where I wanted to be.

I smirked before taking another mouthful of this sweet poison.

CHAPTER SEVEN

The last couple of days with Everly passed quickly and I was excited for my week with Aimee. It was our second time, and this time I felt anxious. There was something about me that was curious about her. She always left me wanting to know more.

I left work at five pm sharp and walked to my Maserati, smiling as I unlocked it. I plugged my phone in and started playing my Motown playlist as I drove away from work. It was only a short drive, but what with it being a Friday the traffic was worse than normal.

As soon as I was home I jumped into the shower, so I was fresh and ready for my evening. I decided we would go out for dinner, just so I could get to know her a little better.

Once out the shower I threw on a pair of black skinny jeans and a fitted khaki tee and my black trainers. I slipped my watch onto my wrist and tousled my mousy hair, finishing off with a spray of cologne.

I poured two glasses of white and waited patiently for

my door to go. She made me nervous and I couldn't understand why. I used to feel nervous with Rylie, but none of the other girls made me feel like this. I rubbed my stubble from my chin to my cheek bone with my hand before jumping up when I heard the door go.

A big grin spread across my face as I saw her walk through the door. Her short blonde hair was styled in beach waves, her face was made up but not over the top. Her black dress clung to her boobs and hips perfectly, she looked amazing.

"Aimee," I purred.

"Carter." She beamed at me. "Nice to see you again." She held her hand out. Taking it, I planted a soft kiss on the back of it.

"Ready for dinner?" I asked her.

"If that's what you want to do," she replied, and I couldn't help but hear the disappointment in her voice.

"Oh, baby, I want to wine and dine you first. Get to know you a little bit better before I have my way with you." My lips twitched at the thought of our after-dinner plans. "I bought you some new underwear, head upstairs to you room and go and slip it on." I winked at her as I picked my keys up off the hallway sideboard.

I watched her blush before she made her way upstairs, I bit my lip as the higher she went, the more of a view I got of her perfectly, peached arse.

Within minutes she was back downstairs, still looking flustered.

"Did it fit alright?" I asked as I placed my hand on the small of her back, gently gesturing for her to start walking.

"What there was of it, yes!" she said with a smirk on her face. I had bought her a black set of crotchless panties and a bralette that covered just her nipples. I calmed my breathing as I thought about her in the set before my lips twisted into a pout to stop myself smirking.

I had booked a reservation at The Ivy, I liked it and always bought the girls here. We were shown to our regular table by our host. I pulled her seat out for her at the restaurant as she took a seat delicately before thanking me. I smiled at her before taking my own seat and ordering us a bottle of wine.

"So, Aimee, tell me about yourself," I pried as I took a mouthful of the wine and nodding in approval of the taste.

"There isn't much to know." She smiled at me while taking a sip, keeping her eyes on me the whole time.

I laughed at her response and shook my head. "Well, what did you wanna be when you grew up?" I asked her, my eyes now on hers.

"Exactly what I am," she teased which made me laugh out loud again.

"Hmm, really? I don't believe that" I said before being interrupted by the waiter. "Would you mind me ordering for you?" I asked her.

"Of course not." She fluttered her lashes at me. God, I wanted her. I ordered two steaks with all the trimmings then turned back to our conversation.

"So, you always wanted to be a well-paid booty call?" I said, my voice full of cockiness.

"Exactly." She bit her lip slightly and shuffled in her seat.

"You didn't want to be a nurse, or a vet or anything else like that?" I teased.

"Okay, fine." she rolled her eyes in a joking matter. "I wanted to be hair dresser, but then once I went to college, I dropped out, it just wasn't for me." She shrugged. "So then I just found myself temping between jobs, and okay it wasn't great money, but it was something new every few weeks." She smiled. "And then, I bumped into you. One of the best days of my life." She winked at me then eyed her food as the waiter served our plates in front of us. She teased me throughout our dinner and by that point, I didn't want anymore. I just wanted her.

I paid the bill and grabbed her hand, dragging her out quickly. The valet bought my car round as I threw him a tip before sliding into the car, her slipping in next to me.

I squeezed her thigh and my car roared as we pulled out onto the main road. I let go and gently trailed my index finger up her thigh slowly, my eyes glistened as I watched her breath catch.

I continued my teasing trial, hitching her dress up with my hand before continuing to the apex of her thighs. I grinned as she opened her thighs slightly, revealing the sexy crotchless panties I told her to change into. I ran my finger up her soaked core, while keeping my eyes on the road the whole time, smirking at how I have made her feel by one touch.

I slowly continued to stroke her, watching her begin to fall apart beneath my touch. Before her breathing gets too fast, I pull myself away before wrapping my fingers around the steering wheel. I look over at her, smirking as I watch her panting, trying to catch her breath.

"All okay?" I ask, knowing full well that she wasn't okay.

"Not really." She panted then realised her dress was still hitched. She frowned and pulled it down, wrapping her leg over the other one.

"And why's that princess?" I teased.

"Because you teased me." She sulked.

"Because I can. You belong to me during this week remember?" I said shaking my head slightly, feeling irritated when I watched her huff.

"You are mine, not the other way around. If I want to get my kicks and leave you hanging, I will. I don't have to give you anything if I don't want to," I said sternly. "Just remember that your orgasms belong to me and only me.

They are a present from me to you, I can give them just as quickly as I can take them away." Burning my sage eyes into hers. "Don't forget any of that princess."

I took my eyes off of hers and concentrated back on the road. This evening had taken a quicker turn than I would have liked, but instead of us just having plain old vanilla sex, we will now have punishment sex.

I pulled into the carpark of my penthouse, neither of us had said a word since which annoyed me. She was acting like a brat. I didn't like brats. I walked round to her side of the car and opened the door for her. As she stepped out I put my arms around her waist, lifting her up then throwing her over my shoulder giving her a firm slap on her arse cheek. She yelped as I done it, but I kept quiet. I was too busy stewing and thinking about how I am going to punish her. I kept hold of her as I walked through to the penthouse.

"Carter put me down!" she shouted at me, smacking me on the back with both of her hands. I ignored her, which only made her more annoyed. I walked into the guest bedroom and threw her down on the bed. Her eyes were alight, and not with passion but with anger.

"Who the fuck do you think you are?" she said as she went to get up. I shook my head up and pushed her gently back down.

"I am your boss. Now undress to your underwear," I demanded. "Then you can lay on the bed and wait till I am ready to use you." I said each word slowly, making sure she understood.

I watched as she stood there, her gorgeous fucking body, her full tits hanging out of the bralette I bought her. She looked fucking delicious.

I stepped close to her, drinking in her scent. I slowly traced my finger from her chin down to her bra, pulling it down and releasing her breast. I groaned before taking it into my mouth, slowly flicking my tongue across her nipple, then sucking it hard. I pulled away and gently blew on her, before taking it back into my mouth and continuing the same rhythm for her.

She was moaning as I continued to pleasure her, her chest moving up and down fast as her panting became heavier. With my free hand I made my way to her soaking core. I smiled against her skin before nipping at her. I slipped two fingers deep inside as I started pushing them deeper while rubbing her soft spot with my thumb.

I planted a soft kiss on her now, over sensitive breasts, and then moved up to meet her eyes, keeping my lips near hers. Her moans started getting louder and I could feel her muscles starting to clamp around my fingers tightly. That was my cue, my cue to pull away.

I slipped my fingers out of her which caused her to whimper at the loss of me, her lips parted where she was trying to catch her breath. I placed my two fingers, covered in her arousal on her bottom lip then slowly forced them into her mouth.

"Suck," I said bluntly. She did just that. Fuck I wanted her lips around me. I pulled them out and winked at her.

"Good girl," I purred. I turned on my heel, a massive grin spread across my face. "I'll be back soon, don't touch yourself."

I walked towards the door, not looking back over my shoulder.

I walked straight into my bedroom, stripping off at the door then stepping under my shower. I liked Aimee a lot, there was something different about her, but I didn't know what. I knew I wasn't falling for her, I don't allow that to happen, but there was something that was making me want so much more with her.

I shook my head as I washed the shampoo off my hair, I needed to remember I just fuck and go. She is just a fuck, and I couldn't wait to bury myself in her. I hopped out the shower and towel dried myself off and my hair before slipping a pair of clean boxers on.

I sprayed some cologne and styled my hair before making my way back into the guest room. I was already hard just thinking about what I was going to do with her. I bit my lip as I slowly opened the door, and there she was, flustered and looking sexy, laying on the bed with her legs slightly parted waiting for me.

"Miss me?" I teased as I walked slowly over to her, her

eyes scanning me from head to toe, her lips open slightly as her breath caught.

I crawled up the bed and straight between her legs, my mouth on hers before she could say anything. Her tongue was hungry, cradling my tongue on every stroke. She had so much pent up sexual frustration that I couldn't wait to release.

As I pulled my mouth away from hers, I took her bottom lip in between my teeth and bit down, a moan escaping her. I moved myself down between her legs as I smiled at her perfectly waxed sex that was still glistening with her arousal from earlier.

I gave her no warning as my mouth was straight onto her, my tongue flicking and nipping at her sensitive spot. I kept my eyes on her, her body writhing on the sheets, bunching them in her clasp. I inserted my fingers into her, her hips started bucking towards me.

"Carter," she whimpered. "Please."

I slipped my fingers out and stood up, smiling down at her. "All okay?" I asked.

"Please, Carter. I need my release," she begged.

"Not yet, sorry, princess. You act like a brat, I treat you like a brat," I snapped, laughing to myself.

"Bend over the bed," I mumble as I walk out the room to get a little something.

I decided on a long, brown leather crop. As I walked into the room I slapped the end of the crop across my hand

and heard her gasp.

"Oh, don't worry, it's not going to hurt."

I walked over to her and run the tip down her spine. She is face down with her perfectly peach arse in the air, displaying her perfect sex. I am so hard for her but I ain't giving into her that easily. She is so wet, I don't know how much longer she is going to be able to hold her orgasm.

I trace the crop down to the base of her spine and run it in-between her cheeks before slapping it against her opening. She moans out load before I do it again. I reach forward and bunch her hair in my hands, pulling her up onto her knees.

This time I trace the soft leather tip along her collar bone, tracing it in-between her breasts then running it gently across her navel. I keep my spare hand splayed across her glistening skin. I plant a gentle kiss on her neck as her breathing changed once the crop made its way to her exposed sex.

Her head rolled back against my chest as I teased her while still planting soft kisses against her skin. I couldn't believe how well she was doing; most girls would have come by now. I pulled her from her moment as I slapped the crop against her over sensitive spot. I smiled as she cried out.

I circled the crop on the inside of her thigh before slapping it there again. A blissful moan escaped her plump lips. One more time then I will let her come. I will finally give her what she has been craving since the car ride home.

I, again, traced the tip of the crop up the other thigh before slapping against her again. Her moan was louder this time. I needed her now. I needed to get my own release as well as give her hers. I wanted to take it from her, that was the plan, but I couldn't. I couldn't be that selfish with her.

I threw the crop on the bed and pushed my boxers down to my ankles, kicking them across the room. She was still on her knees, her back arched slightly, panting. I came up behind her, my large hands holding onto her delicate hips as I pulled her against me slightly, so she could feel me, so she could feel how hard and ready I was for her.

I moved her forward slightly as I knelt behind her, placing my back against the headboard. I could hear her slight whimpers of having me so close to giving her the release she wanted. I teased her by slowly placing myself against her soaked opening, but not giving her it until I was ready.

She placed her hands on my fore arms as she balanced herself, and with that I entered her, hungrily and fierce. She cried out as she finally had the contact she needed, my lips were back on her neck as her head was thrown back towards me, resting on my chest. My hands on her hips as I pulled her into me again and again.

I could feel myself building, she was moaning each time I hit into her as hard as I could. The fact she still had her crotchless panties on was making it even hotter. I felt her tighten around me as a moan left her lips.

"Faster, Carter, I am so close."

"Fuck," I whispered into her ear. "I want you to come for me so hard, princess."

I tightened my grip on her hips as I pulled her into me harder to meet my fast and punishing thrusts into her. Her hands clamped tighter onto my forearms as her hips started to move with mine. I couldn't go any faster, I smashed into her one last time before she came hard, crying and whining out my name. I followed her, coming down from my almighty high. I released her hips, then grabbed her chin with my hand tilting it back so my lips were next to her jaw.

"Well done, princess, fucking perfect," I said in a low husky voice. "Tomorrow will be all about you."

I nipped at her jaw line. She didn't say a word, she was completely undone and exhausted.

"Go get cleaned up and get into bed. I'll see you tomorrow." I moved away from her and watched her collapse into the bed. I leaned over, kissing her on her forehead before walking out the room feeling very satisfied.

She done so well, so the least I can do is repay her with my tongue. I bit my lip at the thought as I made my way into my own bedroom.

CHAPTER EIGHT

The last few months with Aimee passed too quickly. I had become very fond of her. Our sex was amazing, and she actually enjoyed talking to me about my work and trying to get to know me that bit better.

By the time Friday rolled around I was gutted to be having to say goodbye, knowing full well that I wouldn't be seeing her for about four weeks. The four weeks were going to drag. The last couple of weeks she had been a bit more distant, but I put it down to her knowing our time is coming to an end. I shook it off and just thought I was reading into it too much. I helped her downstairs with her suitcase and sat in the kitchen with her at my dining table.

"So, how have you found your last few weeks with me?" I asked as I passed her a cup of tea.

"I loved it, and to be honest, I'm sad to go," she said as she bit her lip. I studied her face; her plump lips and her pale complexion made her blue eyes stand out.

"Want me to be honest back?" I cooed as I pulled myself closer to her. "I've become quite attached to you, princess," I said with a heavy sigh.

She placed her hand over mine and gently rubbed the back of my knuckles.

"Well, seeing as you said that…" her voice trailed off and she looked down at her cup, then shook her head. "No, no forget it," she said with a little laugh.

"No come on, tell me," I pushed.

"I've fallen for you," she said in a whisper. I quickly pulled my hand away from hers and sat back in my chair, my sage eyes fixated on hers.

"No, princess. You haven't," I stuttered. What was wrong with me? I haven't felt like this since Rylie.

"It's true, Carter, I really have," she said taking her bottom lip between her teeth. I didn't want to admit that I was falling for her too, so I done what I knew best. Pushed her away. Became the arsehole that I knew I was.

"It's just a fuck, Aimee," I said bitterly even though my heart was begging for me to stop, but it was too late. The poison from my black and broken heart was seeping through my veins and I couldn't stop it.

"This is the arrangement. You come to me, we fuck. No feelings, you are mine for that week and then you go off and do you," I said with venom in my voice. She looked at me, her eyes glassed over.

"But you said you had become attached to me," she said in a small voice. Yes, yes, I have. But I can't admit it, I can't let myself be vulnerable again. I burned my eyes into hers.

"Yes, attached to the fuck, Aimee. Attached to the fact that I wanted to up your week to two weeks. Attached to the thought of having you at my beck and call and ruining you until you are no use to me," I spat, my eyes on her the whole time. Watching her break right in front of me. My conscious was screaming "you fucking idiot" at me, but I wasn't going there again. This was my arrangement. To have seven girls I fuck.

"You're an arsehole," she said as she stood up. "You owe me two weeks of presents now you prick," she shouted as she threw the cup of tea across the kitchen. I dodged it and watched it smash on the kitchen unit. "I didn't want you anyway!" she said clearly hurt by what I had said. "I want my presents now, I know you stash them upstairs. I won't be coming back so you owe me!" she said, her pale skin now turning red with rage, her eyes hooded.

I didn't say anything. I walked upstairs and entered my walk-in wardrobe and looked at the piles of presents. Each girl's is named and is specifically for their taste. I spotted Aimee's and sighed at the boxes of girls. Hermes, Tiffany, Cartier, Louis Vuitton, Louboutin and Mulberry. I spoiled her the most. Because she was my favourite, and I had fallen for her. And the prick in me couldn't even tell her.

I made my way downstairs with her gifts and placed them in her Mercedes CLC outside. "All in your car," I said, my ego beaten.

"I would say thanks, but you don't deserve it. You can't say you didn't feel what I did, Carter," she said shaking her head as she picked up her bags.

"Aimee, don't do this, come back next month. We are good together like this." I sighed. "You know we are."

She walked past me and slipped into her red convertible. "Yea, we are, but I need more. You aren't willing to give it to me. I know someone who is."

I was seething.

"I will find him, and I will do everything in my power to fucking ruin anyone or anything that stands in my way. Call it revenge, I will get you back, Aimee, I don't care what I have to do to you or him to do it," I shouted as she stormed to her car then sped out of my penthouse carpark and into the distance.

My blood was boiling, who is this person that is going to give her what she wants? No one was getting her, I was going to get her back. I pulled my phone out and called someone who owed me a massive favour.

"Hey, Rogers, it's me. I need you to follow Aimee Wells, I need to know who she is going to see. You might find out tonight, you may not find out till next week, but I want you on her. I want your eyes watching her every move," I snapped before cutting them off.

How fucking dare she. But what did I expect? She made it clear weeks ago how she felt, she was giving me the signs, but I ignored them. Then she told me this morning that she had fallen for me, but like the pussy that I am, I couldn't tell her back. I couldn't tell her that I had fallen for her too, so fucking hard.

A few weeks had passed, and my contact had been back in touch with information on where Aimee had been and who she had been seeing. It was her week back on from tomorrow, but of course she hadn't answered any of my calls and messages.

I went to work and lost myself in the business of my day. I had meeting after meeting, and I was bored shitless listening to the same board members tell me the same stuff.

Friday was just as tedious. I checked my phone constantly to see if she had messaged, but she hadn't.

My phone beeped, my heart thumped into my chest as I unlocked my iPhone, still hoping it was Aimee, but disappointment panged through me when I saw it was Rogers with a name.

Jake Peterson.

He sent me his place of work. I scoffed. He was a mechanic, had his own garage in Elsworth, Cambridgeshire, who she now worked for as a receptionist.

What the fuck did she see in him?

I loosened my light blue tie as I carried on scrolling

through the email link he sent. I couldn't quite see on my phone, so I pinged the link to my computer and started scrolling again. *Oh, Jake Peterson, tut tut.*

I came across a beautiful lady, Freya Greene, who was his fiancée, and he was cheating on her with Aimee. I felt like my heart broke again, I couldn't believe she actually had someone else. My temper was rising. I tried to reason with myself and talk myself down, but I couldn't. I pushed myself away from my chair hard then punched the wall, instantly regretting it. *Fuck.* My knuckles were throbbing. What the fuck did she see in that piss poor excuse of a man?

I felt like breaking him, breaking him like he had broken me. Then it clicked. His fiancée. If I could meet her, take her from him completely, he may feel a snippet of what I am. I grinned to myself as I text Rogers now asking for details on Freya Greene.

I sat back in my chair, staring at her picture, my hands clasped together, my index fingers resting under my chin.

You've met your match Jake Peterson.

CHAPTER NINE

It took a few weeks, but I finally had everything I needed on Freya. She worked in a family run law firm in Elsworth and lived with Jake. Her parents still lived in the same village. I couldn't wait to meet her, and now I had to plan my journey and work out how I was going to accidently *bump* into her.

I started packing an overnight bag, I was planning to head down the weekend coming. I had cancelled the girls I had booked in for this week as I needed a clear head. I went into my bathroom to collect my toiletries. I had booked a small bed and breakfast in Elsworth for a few nights.

I came back and threw the rest of my clothes in my holdall. Normally my house keeper would do all this for me, but I gave her some time off for her family. Julia does so much for me I thought it was only fair that she had some time off.

I checked my phone to see I had missed a call from Rogers, my contact. I cursed and called him back.

"Hey sorry, all okay?" I asked.

"Not really, Cole, there's been a development. Freya isn't at the law firm anymore," he sighed.

"Right, okay, why is that a problem?" I asked confused, my brow furrowed. I didn't know where he was going.

"She is in London," he said bluntly. I choked on his words. What the fuck? She was in *London?*

"How the fuck has that happened?" I snapped at him.

"It seems she has found out about Jake and Aimee," he said quietly.

"Fuck sake," I shouted. "How the fuck am I meant to do this now?" I asked him, I was seething. I could feel the veins in my head pulsing, I knew it wasn't his fault, but I needed to take my frustration out on someone and he seemed a pretty good punching bag at the moment.

"Well, Cole, if you calm down I can tell you," he stuttered.

"Go on," I said, still clearly with a pissed tone in my voice.

"She is working at You Magazine," he said, quietly.

You Magazine? Why did that ring a bell? *Oh, shit.* That's the new magazine I have just taken over.

A smile spread across my face. I looked like a Cheshire cat who had just got the cream.

"Well, isn't this fucking perfect," I said with a laugh. "Fantastic work, Rogers," I said as I sat on the bed. "Even easier for me to get in with her now. She will be heartbroken, and I will be her knight in shining armour to make her feel better. Jake will soon realise what he is missing and come back for her. Then I can see his face when he realises she has fallen for me. Once she has, that's it. I'll leave her broken as well as him. I will get my revenge on Jake with his pretty auburn-haired ex, then Aimee will come running back when she sees how much of a no good mug he is." I smirked. "Bye, Rogers," I said before cutting the phone off.

I pulled up my work calendar to see when I was free to go over and see Jools, the manager who runs You Magazine. I just needed to think of a plan now to get a meeting with Freya.

After my chilled weekend and plotting my next move, it was Sunday evening and I decided to get this plan into motion, so I called Jools.

"Jools. It's Carter." I smiled down the phone. "How is my little business running since I came in and saved you?" I teased her.

"It's running perfectly. I have a new assistant, she started a few weeks back which has helped me out of this ever-growing pile of paperwork." She laughed, and I laughed along with her.

"That's good to hear," I purred. "Jools, I need a

favour," I said, my tone clipped.

"Of course, what can I help you with, Mr Cole?" she asked, her tone going more professional.

"I will be having someone go on long term sick at City Publishing House, would it be cheeky to ask if I could have someone from your team?" I asked, pushing it and I knew it. I could hear Jools sigh in deeply.

"It's going to put me back under it if I'm honest." I heard her tapping her pen on the desk. "But, I suppose I could give you Freya. I'll have to get a temp in. But do me a favour, come over this week to meet her. Give her a challenge and see if you are happy with her. I do give her a hard time, but she is good at her job seeing as she came from a law firm and is completely out of her comfort zone."

My mind was ticking of how I could make her feel out of comfort zone with me, all the things I could get her to do.

"Perfect, Jools. I will come over in the week, tell her that I'm the editor and I want her to get some manuscripts ready. Make sure you are out of the office, so I can gauge her without the pressure of you being there," I said, coming across a lot more bluntly than I would have liked.

"Perfect, how does tomorrow work? Might as well do it on Monday, start the week off right. Two o' clock work for you?" I could hear the smile in her voice

"Fantastic, it's in the diary. I'll see you tomorrow at two, Jools." I put the phone down but not before wishing her a good evening.

I walked into my closet and pulled out my favourite grey suit and white shirt, I couldn't wait to start this little game in winning Aimee back, so I could get her to realise she wants to be with me after Jake runs back to comfort a heartbroken Freya. Now let's see how easily she falls for me.

I woke early, showered and spent a bit more time on my appearance, not that I needed to. Let's be honest, I have women falling at my feet.

I brushed my teeth then styled my hair before staring at myself in the mirror. I couldn't wait to bring her down. I walked downstairs to find Julia finishing my breakfast.

"Morning, Julia." I smiled at her as her eyes met mine.

"Morning, Mr Cole." She smiled back at me.

"It's Carter, please," I said before sitting down at the dining room table. I hung my grey suit jacket on the back of the chair, I didn't want it getting creased for my first meeting with Freya. I watched Julia as she placed my omelette down in front of me.

"Busy day at work today?" she asked. I laughed to myself, she asks me the same questions every morning.

"Yes, quite busy. Meeting a potential client this afternoon which is exciting. What about you?" I always tried to make her feel comfortable, and she was a friend now. She has been working for me for so long, I always felt like I owed her so much for all she does.

I finished my breakfast before placing in the sink, and I saw her eyeball me as I done it.

"I can do it myself, honestly, woman." I laughed at her. "I'll see you tonight for dinner."

I smiled before closing the door. I decided I would get James, my driver, to take me to work today. I wanted a clear mind and I find it's better when I don't drive.

"Morning, James," I said as I slid into the back of the car.

"Morning, Carter," he mumbled as he closed the door behind me before sitting in the front and pulling out the carpark.

I felt nervous, but excited to meet Freya.

After a short car ride we pulled up outside Cole's Enterprise. I thanked James and made my way up to my office before my ten am meeting. I just wanted to be there now, I didn't want to be here.

Finally, one pm rolled around, I was starving. The meeting dragged on a lot longer than needed, but I couldn't be seen to show no interest seeing as we were in the process of trying to bag one of our biggest clients yet, over in New York.

I jumped in the car with James who had kindly picked me up a cheeseburger and milkshake to eat on the way to You Magazine.

"How's your day been, James?" I asked after finishing a mouthful of my food.

"Not bad, boss, done everything you asked. What about you?" he looked in his rear view mirror as he waited for my answer.

"Yea, my day has been good, busy in meetings. This burger has made me day." I chuckled. "Now off for another meeting then hopefully an early finish for us both." I smiled at him as I took a big sip of the milkshake.

"Love an early finish, boss." He grinned at me in the mirror. "You have a massive grin on your face, is there any reason or is that burger really just that good?" He laughed out loud at me.

"The burger is immense, James, not going to lie, *but* I am going to see a new client, hopefully." I bit my lip as I looked down at my phone.

"Busy in the business world at the moment aren't you! Which is great for you," he said as he slowed outside You Magazine's office.

"Oh no, James, this one is purely *pleasure,*" I said, my eyes hooded over as I stepped onto the pavement. "James, could you wait outside for me please, I shouldn't be no more than an hour." I nodded as I done my button up on my suit jacket before making my way into the building.

I walked into the spacious reception area and noticed a petite, young girl staring up at me as I approached her desk.

"Good Afternoon," I said silkily, and her mouth dropped open, unable to say a word while she took me in. I just kept my smile plastered over my face. I loved having this effect on women.

"Can I help you?" she said quietly after a few minutes of her silence, her eyes still fixated on me.

"Yes, yes you can. I am here to see a Miss Freya Greene; my name is Mr Cole," I replied with inquisitiveness in my voice.

"Oh, okay, I will call up to her. Excuse me please," she said as she picked up the receiver, her eyes not leaving mine. I took a step back to give her some privacy but could still hear her tame voice as she started talking.

"Hey," I heard her whisper. "There is an extremely good-looking man in reception asking for you. He says he has a meeting with you at two pm, a Mr Cole."

I laughed quietly to myself as she clung onto the handset.

"Of course, see you in five," she said before putting the phone down. She stood from her desk, her petite, slim frame walking towards me. "Erm, Mr Cole, would you like a drink? I need to grab Freya a coffee, and it would be my pleasure to make you one once you are upstairs," she said.

"Just a water if you wouldn't mind please," I purred back at her as I followed her to the lift.

Within seconds the doors pinged open and I was taken into a small area. I saw what I am assuming was Freya's desk to the right, Jools' office in front with an amazing view of the city thanks to her floor to ceiling windows, and to the left was an all glass meeting room.

I followed the receptionist like a lost puppy as she opened the door and led me into the room.

"Freya, I will be back in a minute with your coffee," she said as she fidgeted before walking to leave the room.

"Thank you, Rachel. Mr. Cole, it's a pleasure to meet you, I'm Freya." Her scent hit my nose, it was so intoxicating that it made me want to get so much closer to her.

My eyes trailed up her body, her legs were long but thick. She had curvaceous hips and a peach of a bum. She had a tiny little waist I would be worried I would snap her. Then her breasts were large, but not too large. They suited her delicate figure perfectly.

I smirked as I saw her trying to discreetly pull her leather pencil skirt down. My eyes continued to her upper body, her sun kissed olive skin was glistening under the lights, her white sleeveless shirt clung to her curves and sat neatly tucked into her skirt, the top buttons slightly open, showing my eyes just enough.

I was pulled away when she came close to me and shook my hand.

"And it's a pleasure to meet you, Freya, please, call me Carter," I purred, my eyes meeting hers. They were a beautiful grey that complimented her skin tone perfectly. I knew she was good looking from her photos, but she was fucking beautiful in person.

Her plump lips were parted slightly, her long auburn

hair was in loose curls that tumbled down past her chest. I wanted to kiss her, right here, right now. I didn't care where I was, I just wanted to lose myself in her. I felt my heartbeat quickening at the thought. *What the fuck.*

"Please take a seat, Carter."

I did as she said, undoing my suit jacket before sitting in front of her. I slipped my iPhone out of my pocket and faced it face down on the table, so I didn't have any distractions. I watched her, her eyes darting over my every feature as if she was trying to drink every ounce of me in. I smirked as her eyes met mine, a blush running over her face at being caught.

"So, how did you feel when Jools asked you to cover for us?" I asked trying to break the clear, sexual tension between us. I wanted her, I could have easily bent her over the table with her leather skirt hitched up over her perfect arse and her fuck me Louboutin's up around my waist.

I shuffled in my seat uncomfortably trying to calm what was happening in-between my legs. I watched her clear her throat before speaking.

"I was a little surprised if I'm honest."

I laughed at her remark. She came across so confident for someone who has had her heart broken and trust betrayed recently.

"Well, I asked her for someone who was hardworking, focused and was good at their job, and she mentioned you," I said trying to reassure her.

"Really?" she said with shock evident in her voice, I looked at her with confusion all over my face. how could she not take a compliment like that?

"Yes, really!" I replied, trying to make her see how serious I was.

I watched her blush from head to toe again, and all I could think of was how I could make her blush in so many other ways.

"I was wondering why you attended the meeting and not your editor?" she asked me, throwing me, which made me realise now that she had obviously done her research on me. Clever girl.

I sat, looking at her smugly before answering. "Because I can. I love reading, and I love finding new writers. Jools mentioned you had an aspiration to write, so I thought I would meet you personally to see if I can get a real feel for the manuscripts you have chosen."

Nice save, Cole.

She was just staring at me. I sat waiting for some sort of response from her, but the petite little receptionist busted back in the room, tearing her eyes from mine. Something was happening, I felt like she was setting my soul alight, re-igniting my feelings.

"Here we go, a coffee for you, Freya, and a water for Mr Cole," she said as she placed the cups down on the table

"Please, Carter." I flashed her my biggest grin which also turned her the same shade of red as Freya. I laughed to myself as she quickly rushed out the room and into the lift.

"So, where were we?" I asked before losing myself in her stunning eyes and listening to her easy conversation and her love of the manuscripts she had chosen for me.

I was intrigued to read them now, just because she had taken the time to actually find something that interested her and thought they would interest me. I saw her check her phone, and I took that as my cue to leave as she stood. I stood with her. I buttoned my suit jacket back up before taking her hand in mine and giving hers another shake, and this time I held on a bit longer.

I couldn't ignore the spark that coursed through my veins. I went to say something to her, trying to make a pass at her but I couldn't find the words to say so decided against it.

A few moments passed before I decided to ask her what I actually came here for; her number so I could get the ball rolling on my plan.

"I was wondering, can I take your number? Just easier so I don't have to go through reception or await a response by email."

I saw her pick her phone up, smiling. "Of course," she said in response before we exchanged numbers.

I walked with her to the lift, watching her the whole time, and my heart melted a bit as I saw her clenching the manuscripts tightly to her chest.

"Well, it was lovely meeting you, Carter. I will be sure

Jools gets these manuscripts tonight. I already have put another three on her desk, so I am sure she will be in contact with you, and again, it was lovely to meet you."

I watched as she tried to calm her breathing. I didn't want to leave, I didn't want to go and have to wait to see her again. There was something going on between us. The feeling was alien to me, I felt like my heart had swelled in my chest. I knew how I felt with Rylie, but I couldn't explain this. She was like a drug, I felt addicted to her and she was the only one who could cure this need. I still wanted to get the plan in motion, but part of me was regretting it already. I ignored the second feeling before taking my phone out of my pocket and pushed the button to call the lift.

"You too, Freya," Her name slipped off my tongue too easily. I stepped into the lift, watching her tuck her gorgeous auburn hair behind ear.

I pressed the ground floor button before saying, "Goodbye, Freya," as the doors shut on me.

I finally let out the breath I didn't realise I had been holding, my heart thumping through my chest. *What the fuck was that?* I needed to get home, I needed to fuck something to get that stunning, heartbreakingly beautiful woman out of my head.

I was grateful to see James sitting parked outside waiting for me. He clambered out the car and opened my door as I got in, loosening my tie, throwing my head back and taking a couple of deep breaths.

"Good meeting?" James asked as we started to drive.

"Fantastic," I said, still a little out of breath. God, I need to see her again. My thumb hovered over her number, but I talked myself out of it. Maybe I would contact her tomorrow. If I could wait that long.

CHAPTER TEN

I paced my hallway between the front door and the living room, waiting for Everly to come over. I didn't even want to see her, yet I needed to get Freya out of my head.

How could a lousy meeting that I only arranged to start my plan have such an effect on me? I could feel myself getting annoyed. Annoyed that I had let myself get so caught up by her. I sighed in relief when I heard the buzzer go, letting me know that someone was making their way up in the lift.

I stood waiting for her, still in my now creased grey suit. I threw my tie off in frustration as soon as I got in James' car after my meeting with Freya I looked at myself in the hallway mirror, my eyes wrinkled at the side.

I had noticeable lines on my forehead from where my expression had been in a constant frown since my meeting. I relaxed slightly when I saw Everly's long legs walking towards me. Her tiny frame was hidden underneath a plain white tee, her long blonde hair cascading down her back. As soon as her foot was in my hallway I crashed my mouth into hers, my hands up round her face and round the back of her head, entwining my fingers in her locks.

"Woah, somebody missed me?" she purred as she ran her fingers up my forearm.

"Shhh, stop talking," I said in a hushed voice before dragging her through to the guest room.

I slammed the door shut as I pushed her towards the bed. She tried to kiss me, but I didn't want her lips on me. I didn't want to feel her skin on mine. I pushed her forward, so she was facing the bed, her face down in the quilt. I pushed her skirt up round her hips, then wrapped my fingers round the delicate black, silk material of her panties before ripping them from her.

A small whimper left her mouth when she realised exactly what was going to be happening. She knew this wasn't about her.

I undid my button to my suit trousers and kicked them down my legs and off across the other side of the room. I pulled my boxers down just past my thighs and smashed myself into her. I heard her scream as my rough entrance was a shock for her. It didn't feel great for me either.

I didn't care that she wasn't ready for me.

I just wanted to use her to my advantage.

I needed to just fuck her to try and get Freya out of my head.

I didn't let up this brutal and relentless rhythm that I

had going on. I was forceful, maybe a bit too forceful. I leant forward and grabbed her hair tightly in my clutches, pulling her head back. I smirked as I heard small moans leaving her lips, but I wasn't going to let her come.

I closed my eyes trying to block her moans out, but all that did was let me visualise Freya. My breath caught as my imagination let me see her and only her.

My mind was tricking me. It wasn't Everly bent over in front of me, it was Freya. Her long, curly auburn hair was loose and fierce. Her damp, sun kissed skin alight due to my touch. Her perfect moans escaping her plump lips while moaning my name. Her grey eyes finding mine while full of ecstasy as she looked over her shoulder watching me.

I moaned her name in my mind, and it sounded like heaven on my tongue. It slipped off like pure silk. I could feel myself building as my pent up release climbed.

A few more thrusts before I felt myself lose everything. I was bought round from my sweet fantasy by Everly. My face scolded as she bought me back down from my delicious high.

"Carter!" she screeched. "Fucking answer me."

I blinked a few times, trying to register what the fuck was going on. I felt dazed.

"What!?" I snapped back at her, my eyes trying to focus on my surroundings. Everly was sitting on the bed crossed legged, rage all over her face. Her eyes filled with anger.

"What do you mean, what?! You basically just fucked

me to get your own, but to top it off you were calling out *Freya*. Who the fuck is she and why are you calling her name out while you come?" she asked, her eyes boring into mine.

I must have looked dumbstruck as I tried to muster the words. I had so much going around in my head; my brain and mouth weren't registering. I couldn't say what I wanted to say, and with that I snapped.

"Fuck!" I shouted in frustration. "Just fuck off, Everly. We are done. Your contract is terminated with immediate effect," I said angrily, my fists balled.

"What do you mean 'terminated?'" she said quietly, confusion all over her face.

"Exactly that. Now leave. I am done," I said sternly, my eyes on the floor. I couldn't even look at her. I was ashamed. Ashamed of myself and for letting myself get spell bound by Freya. She had put me under her spell, completely and utterly under it. I opened my eyes to see Everly stomping around the bedroom before flipping me her finger and slamming the door behind me.

"Fuck," I muttered before flopping on the bed. Freya has taken over me. Taken over my senses. I laid staring at the ceiling hoping to be pulled from this funk, but nothing was happening. I punched down onto the mattress as I got up and walked into my office. I needed to lose myself working, otherwise I would find out where Freya lived and go over there to live out the fantasy I just had in my head.

A few hours passed and after managing ten minutes of actual work, I had to message Freya. I couldn't not. I scrolled through my phone to find her number. My thumb hovered for a while over it before I bit the bullet and wrote a quick message. I was hoping she was asleep, but at the same time I wanted to hear from her right away.

I hope I didn't wake you, I just haven't been able to stop thinking about you. When are you free? I would love to take you out? Carter X

My heart was racing as I clicked send, not giving it a second thought. I clutched onto my phone as I waited for a response.

Get your head back in the game, Cole. She is just a chick, you have plenty of them that make you feel this way. Don't you? I growled at my subconscious. I knew I didn't have anyone who made me feel like she did.

Maybe it was because I knew what I was going to be doing to her. My head was messed up. I need to stick back to the plan. I need to break her and Jake, so he can realise how he made me feel going with Aimee and offering her something that I didn't get the chance to give her.

Did I want to be in a serious relationship with Aimee?

At the moment, fuck no.

In the future? Possibly.

But now he has taken that away from me and I can't do anything about it except snap Freya's faith and love, then crumble her heart into dust that cannot be repaired by anyone. I want him to see her hurting, I want him to grovel for her back, then that way I can swoop in and take Aimee off of him.

As I thought about my little plan over and over in my head, I was wondering if this was what I wanted to do? I felt like I was constantly battling with myself.

I was soon snapped from arguing with my thoughts as my phone beeped.

A smile I had no control over spreading across my face as I saw her name flash on my screen

No, didn't wake me. I would like that. I'm free whenever. Now with this extra work I have been given, my social life is now extinct. You let me know when is good for you. Goodnight Mr. Cole, sweet dreams X

My dick twitched at the written words '*Mr. Cole*'. I thought back to the first time I heard those two words slip from her lips and off of her tongue. All I could think about was her screaming them as I fucked her senseless. I laughed at her smart comment about not having a social life because of me. Good. I'm glad she isn't going to have one because that means she can't go out and meet anyone as she will be with me, and when she is not, I'll be so deep in her head she won't be able to think of anyone else. I typed a quick response back to her before turning my phone on silent.

Oh I will. Goodnight Miss Greene X

I walked into my bedroom, still in my pants from earlier with Everly. I hadn't heard from her but to be honest, why should I? I slid them down my legs and threw them in the wash basket before stepping under the shower.

I could feel my heart thumping. I couldn't shake this feeling from the pit of my stomach. I know I can be an arsehole, but this is unlike me. The way I treated Everly was uncalled for earlier, but Freya is bringing out a side of me that I never knew existed.

I placed both hands on my dark slate tiles and bowed my head as I let the water cascade over me. I couldn't let this girl get inside my head. It's all because I know it's a game, and a hard one at that. Freya doesn't seem like the girl to want to give it up easily, and it's going to be a task.

I lift my head slowly as the shower water is now hitting me in the face. I thought about how she sat down opposite me, clearly affected by my presence. Her full lips parted, her breathing faster but quiet, her big grey eyes flitting from mine and to my other facial features. All I could think about was her lips round me, savouring my taste.

I grunted as I shut the water off. I wrapped a towel

round my waist and walked out into the bedroom. I pulled open my drawers in my walk-in wardrobe and slipped a clean pair of Calvin Klein pants on. I rough dried my hair before throwing my towel on the floor of the en-suite. I couldn't be bothered to hang it up, I was in a shit mood.

I ran downstairs, grabbing a bottle of bourbon and making my way back upstairs. Sod the glass. I threw myself on the bed and took a big sip of the brown poison that ran down my throat like pure silk, the burn making me wince.

I didn't stop. I took another two then leant over and grabbed my earphones off of the side and put them in as I flicked through my playlist. I couldn't switch off, I needed some of my music to send me into a restful sleep.

I scoffed at my stupidity. I knew I wouldn't be sleeping tonight. I threw back another big swig before placing the bottle on my bedside table. I sat brooding for a while as I felt the brown, hard liquor burn through my veins, setting them alight with the alcohol coursing through them.

I needed to get my head straight in the morning. I'll give Louis a call and see if he can snap me out of being a pussy over someone I only met for a couple of hours. I think I'll go out with Freya Friday, see how it goes. See if I can seduce her enough to get into her panties, make her fall so fucking hard for me. Should only take a week at most then I can shatter her beneath my touch.

I'll tell her about my 'flavours.' That's one thing that will scare her away. I bit my lip thinking about it all as I hit play on *Found You – Austin Mahone.* I instantly relaxed as his voice echoed through my ears.

It wasn't long before my eyes fell heavy and everything went black around me.

CHAPTER ELEVEN

My alarm went off at six am, and I hit it in temper. I was awoken before it and frustrated that, as expected, I didn't sleep as much as I wanted too. I staggered to my bathroom and splashed myself with cold water, trying to wake myself up.

I moped downstairs and put the coffee machine on. Julia was nowhere to be seen which annoyed me even more. I grabbed my hot cup and made my way over to my sofa overlooking the city. It felt weird waking up alone. I normally have one of my girls here. I can't remember the last time I woke up alone, the last time I felt alone.

"Morning, Carter," I heard Julia's bright, chirpy voice bellow through the rooms.

"Morning, Julia," I grunted back at her, my eyes fixated on my stunning view.

"Everything okay? You not feeling well?" she asked as she stood in the entrance way to the living room. I felt my face soften, and my mood lift slightly.

ASHLEE ROSE

"I'm okay, didn't sleep great. How are you?" I asked as I turned slightly to face her.

"I am fine, thank you for asking." She smiled. "I'll start breakfast for you and Everly, is it the usual?" she asked clasping her hands together.

"It's just me, Julia, and will be for the rest of the week," I said as I pulled my eyes from hers.

"Oh," I heard her say. "Okay, no problem. Omelette?" she asked sweetly.

"Please," I mumbled back at her.

"Be ready in ten, with a fresh coffee." She smirked at me. She knew I always made shit coffee. I smirked as I bought it up to my lips and pulled a face as the bitterness hit my tongue. God that was truly shocking. I lugged myself off of the sofa and made my way to the kitchen, pouring the thick, tar like coffee down the sink.

I was thirty three, how could I not make a cup of coffee? I sat at the breakfast bar watching Julia work her way around the kitchen.

"Will it just be you for dinner tonight?" she asked, keeping her eyes on the omelette she was cooking. She actually was a saint, I don't know what I would do without her.

"Yes," I said, sighing.

"Are you sure you're okay? I don't want to intrude, and I am sorry if I am overstepping the mark, but I have never seen you like this," she said with concern all over her face, sliding me a fresh brewed cup of coffee.

"I don't know," I said quietly, looking down at my cup, watching the steam rise. "I am lonely, I've hardly slept so that isn't helping." I shrugged at her. She gave me a sympathetic smile and placed her hand over mine.

"You won't be alone forever, I can promise you that," she said hushed. "You aren't destined to grow old by yourself." She smiled as she went back and plated my breakfast. "Now eat up, and I'll see you at dinner," she said as she placed the frying pan in the dishwasher.

"Thank you, Julia, really," I said before taking a mouthful. I watched as she left the room and shook my head at myself.

Today is a new day, let's start a fresh. I finished my breakfast, placed my plate and fork into the dishwasher and made my way to the shower. I left for the office early with James, I had a busy day full of meetings which I was happy for in a way as it kept my mind busy and focussed instead of moping around.

I was glad to see my watch say five p.m. It had been a long day with back to back meetings. I slid into the back of the car and headed home. Me and James lost ourselves in small chatter while sitting in the evening rush hour of London.

I wished James a good night and made my way into the kitchen where my dinner was sitting on the dining room table. My belly grumbled in appreciation seeing as I hadn't eaten since this morning.

I flicked through my calendar on my phone to work out what day would be best to meet Freya. It was already Wednesday, so I thought Friday would be an ideal 'date night.'

Before I text her, I dropped Louis a text asking him to call me when he had five minutes. I rolled my eyes as I sent it, knowing full well he wouldn't call for a few days. I got changed into my jogging bottoms and lazed on my sofa flicking through the channels while enjoying a cold beer. Even though I slept so bad last night I didn't feel tired. I stopped flicking once I come across the film 'See No Evil, Hear No Evil.' I loved this film.

It was gone eleven by the time the film finished, and I finally felt sleepy. I definitely felt better about everything than I did this morning. I picked my phone up and ignored the number of unread work emails I had and clicked straight onto Freya's name

Hey, how does this Friday work for dinner? I look forward to it.
Carter X

I waited for it to send and saw that it hadn't been delivered. I shrugged it off and walked towards the kitchen to throw my empty bottle away. I grabbed a glass and poured an ice-cold glass of water then made sure the penthouse was locked up before making my way up to bed. I was glad that I actually felt dead on my feet. Maybe I would sleep better than I did last night. I needed a good night's sleep seeing as my first meet up with Freya was Friday. I didn't want to look like Mr Teddy tired eyes.

My alarm woke me from a deep slumber. I felt like I had been asleep for weeks. I rolled and hit the off button. Freya still hadn't messaged back so I thought I would drop her another message. It was five forty-five, but surely she would be up soon for work.

Freya, I didn't hear back from you? I hope you are ok, Carter X

Before dragging myself to get ready for another hectic day at the office, I checked my phone and smiled as it beeped, flashing her name across my screen.

Hey, you, Friday is perfect. Let me know details when you can. Sorry for the no reply last night, I switched my phone off, just needed some quiet time.
Freya X

I was glad to have heard from her, and so excited for

Friday. I can't wait to wine and dine her. I dropped her one last message as I pulled up outside the office.

I can't wait, will send the details soon, Carter X

-

I was so glad that Friday was finally here. I had been excited all day. I ran home quickly to shower. I arranged for a bouquet of a dozen white roses to be sent to Freya's address that I managed to get off of our system seeing as she was now enrolled under my payroll. I wrote a note on the card telling her I would pick her up at eight. I had butterflies, but I think it was more apprehension as to how the evening was going to go.

I slipped into tailored black suit trousers and matched it with a crisp white shirt. I unbuttoned the top two buttons, so it looked a bit more casual. I sprayed my cologne, brushed my teeth and styled my hair with hair clay giving it the 'tousled' look. I think I had had the same hairstyle since college, but it was easy and simple and not very much too it.

I slipped my watch on and grabbed my phone off the side, it was seven-fifteen, perfect. I ran downstairs and met James at the front door and smiled at him as I grabbed my matching suit jacket. I adjusted my cuffs of my sleeves, so they were pulled down just before the suit sleeve finished.

"Looking very dapper, Mr Cole," he teased.

"Thanks, James, hot date." I winked at him entering

the car.

The car journey took a bit longer than I would have liked. I constantly looked at my watch, I didn't want to be late for our first date. I sighed in relief as we finally pulled up outside her apartment block.

The area looked run down, I didn't like the fact that she lived here. I took a deep breath as I got out of the car and made my way up to the block. The communal door was ajar which annoyed me even more, any tramp could just walk into here.

I jogged up the stairs and stood outside her door, my heart felt like it was going to rip out my chest. One more deep breath before knocking on the door, my eyes soft as I waited for her to answer the door when I heard her shout out "*one second!*"

I smirked and looked at my feet as I waited for her. The door swung open and my mouth dropped open, she looked sensational.

Her auburn curls tumbled down past her breast, her make-up was natural and not caked on like some girls I have dated, she wore a light, white floral dress that sat just past her knees, the dress clung to her curves perfectly.

I bit my lip as the soft sleeves sat off of her tanned shoulders and dropped slightly by her, not over exposed, cleavage. I couldn't get over how amazing she looked. I met her eyes as I watched them look me up and down slowly, her lips parted as she took me in and I gave her my best smile.

"Hello, Freya, you look – I mean you've always looked beautiful when I've seen you, but you look amazing."

I watched as she crossed her legs before blush spreading all across her face. She looked back up at me, with her beautiful smile plastered across her face.

"Thank you for the beautiful flowers Carter." She looked over her shoulder and admired the flowers I sent that were sitting on her kitchen side.

"You are welcome, beautiful flowers for a beautiful woman – you ready?" I asked her. She nodded at me and stepped out the front door. I took her hand in mine and held it tightly as we walked down the stairs and out to James waiting for us.

I let go of her hand. "After you," I said as I watched as she slid into the back of the car. I smiled as she thanked James for holding her door open. I leant over and gave her a kiss on her cheek and felt something course through me. I shook it off then placed my hand on her leg and give her a small squeeze.

I loved watching the effect I had on her. I looked her up and down, undressing her with my eyes.

"A glass of champagne?" I asked her, and she nodded eagerly as I poured the bottle of Dom Perignon 2006 from the cooler. "I'm looking forward to tonight," I muttered, smirking at her as I passed her a glass.

CHAPTER TWELVE

I couldn't take my eyes off of her the whole car journey. I could see I was intimidating her, but I just couldn't stop looking at her. I tried to ease her by chatting about work but assured her work talk would stop as soon as we got to the restaurant.

After fifteen minutes of light chatter we pulled up outside The Ivy, one of my favourite restaurants. I always bring my 'flavours' here to chat about terms and what I expect of them. James opened our door, I stepped out before Freya, doing my suit jacket button up before leaning down and taking her small hand to help her out. I pulled her close to me, taking in her scent.

"I will call you when we are finished, James." He nodded at me before getting back in the car and driving away. I saw the queue and rolled my eyes at the people waiting as I briskly walked up to the host on the door. I placed my hand on the small of her back. I tried to contain my smile as I could see how I affected her.

"Evening, Mr Cole, please follow me," the host muttered as he led us through. I ushered her in front of me as I kept close behind her, scouring the room for any of my flavours.

I have cancelled all my girls this month as I just wanted to focus on Freya. I sighed in relief when I couldn't see anyone.

"We have your usual table set up and ready for you, Sir."

I nodded at Marius as I pulled Freya's chair out.

"After you, Freya, thank you, Marius, that will be all." Marius nodded at me and walked back into the hustle and bustle of the restaurant. I sat staring at her, keeping my sage eyes on hers the whole time when I noticed the waitress walking over to us asking what we would like to drink, all the time keeping her eyes on me with a stupid grin across her face.

"We will take a bottle of the Condrieu please," I snapped shutting the menu, handing it back to the waitress.

"Perfect," she chirped, still grinning at me. I just wanted her to leave instead of loitering around me. I kept my eyes on Freya the whole time, not wanting to give this waitress any unwanted attention.

"How's your day been?" I asked. I rolled my eyes when I saw the waitress appear and pour a glass of wine for both myself and Freya. I saw Freya watching the waitress before turning her eyes back on mine.

"It wasn't too bad to be honest, being kept busy by certain people." She smirked as she took her eyes away from mine before flicking them back up at mine. "But I did get to leave early as I worked through my lunch, so I could head to the shops," she said as she mirrored me taking a sip of the wine. I loved this wine.

I placed my glass down before speaking. "Well, you tell whoever is keeping you busy to back off," I said smiling at her. "What did you buy? Something new for tonight?" I teased her.

She got flustered slightly before replying. "I did actually, yes, everything I am wearing is new, thought I would treat myself."

I tilted my head to study her, then I looked down to her dress. "Well, I must admit you chose very well, you look breath taking." And I wasn't lying. She was an actual goddess.

I knew I was in some deep shit with her, even though I knew the plan I felt myself not wanting to go ahead with it the more I spent time with her. She snapped me from my thoughts when she started to speak.

"So, tell me about you, Mr Cole," she asked as she tucked into her seabass. I loved a girl that ate and didn't push their food round their plate. She took a big gulp of her white wine. I had moved onto a red Santenay to compliment my steak.

I looked up at her. "I like it when you call me by my last

name, Miss Greene," I said, teasing her. "What would you like to know?" I watched as she put her knife and fork down and topped her wine up from the bottle chiller.

"Where are you from? I can't help but hear that little twang when you talk?" I couldn't help it, but I laughed out loud. A deep belly laugh, and my god it felt amazing to laugh. I couldn't remember the last time I laughed like that.

"That twang, Miss Greene is Australian. I'm originally from Adelaide." I watched as a shocked expression came across her beautiful face.

"Wow, Australia, I've never been but would love to visit. What made you move to London?" she asked, so intrigued. Oh boy, I didn't want to delve into too much, I needed to keep her at arm's length. I can't let her get that close. I took a big mouthful of my red wine as I shuffled uncomfortably in my seat before speaking.

"We moved to London when I was eighteen, my father wanted to expand Cole Enterprises over to the UK after buying a few struggling firms here, mainly shipping yards and boat manufacturers, so we followed him. I still go back from time to time to make sure our company is a success back in Adelaide, but I'm mainly here. I have an apartment over there, and my parents' house is still there. They didn't want to sell it." I cleared my throat as I knew I was going to start speaking about my father.

"My mum likes to go back over there, but she doesn't like travelling alone so she normally waits for my sister to visit then flies back with her. My sister, Ava, heads up our business back home, but both are solely owned by me, being the first born and only son." I wanted to stop talking but I couldn't, her eyes darted back and forth from mine. She looked so invested in my conversation.

I wanted to put a lid on it, but it felt so good to talk to someone who was generally interested in me and my life for once. I continued, "My father passed the companies over to me when he was taken ill." I shuffled again in my seat, I could feel myself getting choked. I swallowed the lump back down without her noticing my reaction.

"Oh, Carter. I am so sorry," she said sympathetically, her brow furrowed slightly making her eyebrows nearly touch, her eyes glassed over.

I took her hand. "It's okay, it was nine years ago now that he passed." I saw the look on her face change, she felt sorry for me.

My wounded, broken heart hurt. How could she sense that from just me talking? Had I let my wall down that much already?

I let go of her hand in a panic and straightened myself up as I continued to eat.

"Now tell me about you, what's your life story?" I watched as she was clearly uncomfortable. I knew all about her life, I just wanted to hear her side of it.

She took another bite of her seabass before talking. "Well, there isn't much to know. I am originally from

Elsworth, Cambridgeshire where I worked for a family law firm, then I decided to move to London after being offered a job at You Magazine." Nicely dodged Miss. Greene, I thought to myself.

I called her out on it seeing as I knew why she really up and left. "Why would you just decide one day to move from your home town to London?" I smirked as she pushed her gorgeous locks behind her ear, her chest was starting to go red, she was getting flustered.

"Well, I just wanted to move away, become independent." I laughed out at her poor excuse of a story.

"I'm not buying it. Who were you running from?" I egged her on. Come on Freya baby. Stop lying to me. I know it all already sweetness. I watched as she rolled her eyes.

"An ex, it was hardly running, I caught him cheating. My best friend lived here and managed to get me a job at You Magazine, so I really had nothing to stay for." She was clearly nervous telling me about this, I felt a pang of sadness and regret rip through me. I just wanted to scoop her up and tell her no one would ever hurt her again, but I would be lying to her. Because she was going to get hurt again, she was going to get hurt by me.

I put my best confused look on for her behalf. "Why on earth would anyone cheat on you?" I asked. She shrugged my question off while holding tightly onto her wine glass stem before she started talking.

"He had his reason, obviously. He's now engaged and

moving to London because she's been offered a job here." She let out a big breath, my mind was going crazy.

Aimee was engaged?! Fucking engaged to him, a nobody.

My blood boiled. I wanted to rage and throw everything off of the table, but I couldn't. I needed to keep my cool. I needed Freya to think I was on her side in all of this. To think that this wasn't killing me on the inside.

She looked up from her hands and caught my eyes. I could lose myself in them. They were a beautiful grey pool that I just wanted to dive in and get lost.

Snap the fuck out of it, Carter, stick to the fucking plan.

"He is an idiot, but his loss is my gain." I smiled at her, even though I was dying inside.

"Anyway, let's move away from my life and back to yours," she said. I shook my head.

"Nope, let's not talk about our lives anymore, do you fancy getting out of here? We can go back to my place for a drink?" I asked her. I wanted to see if she would give in, to see how easy she would give herself up to me. She looked uneasy at my question, I knew she wouldn't be the type to jump straight into bed, and I admired her for it. I was to used to women throwing themselves on my dick.

"I'm not sure," she said. "I have a bridesmaid fitting tomorrow, early."

I stopped her talking. "I promise, just one drink –

that's it." I pushed her again. Come on baby. Don't give into me. This is all a test. I watched as she looked at her phone screen, obviously checking the time.

"Okay, one drink," she said as she slipped her phone in her bag. And just like that she gave into me. Maybe I was wrong about her. *Fuck.*

I signalled the waitress over to settle the bill, I needed to get out of here now. I needed to think with my head and not my dick for once.

I saw Freya look up, her face dropping as she focussed on something coming up behind us. *Shit, Everly was here.* She approached the table and purred my name.

"Carter."

I looked at her and smiled. "Evening," I muttered back to her as she signalled and mouthed, 'Call me'.

It took me a moment to come back round, she was fucking delicious, but I couldn't go back there. Once a contract was terminated, I was done. I looked at Freya, she had worry all over her face. It's like she was fighting with her thoughts, and I quickly tried to re-assure her.

"Hey, you have nothing to worry about, she's just…" I paused for a moment, thinking this next bit through, "Some girl," I said.

The waitress saved me by arriving with our bill. I saw Freya reach down to get her bag but I shook my head. No way was she paying for her half, I was going to completely ruin her in the next few weeks, so paying for dinner was the least I could do.

"I don't think so, gentlemen don't let their ladies pay." Oh I was so swoon worthy, I could be an actor. I threw my black AmEx down then signed my card receipt. I gave James a quick drop ring, so he knew we were ready.

"Come on, beautiful, I've called James, he will be out front in five".

We waited outside the restaurant, the cool air nipped at my skin. She must be cold; her shoulders were exposed. I took my jacket off and wrapped it round her shoulders before nuzzling my face into her hair. She smelt divine. I couldn't work out what the perfume was, but that mixed with her scent was completely intoxicating.

James pulled up a few moments later, and I didn't want to be taken from this moment. I forgot about everything, I was so caught up in the moment I didn't want it to end. I let go of her, taking her hand and walked her to the car. I let her slide in before I sat next to her.

I watched as she delicately took my suit jacket off and placed it over her lap, covering herself. I sat with my back against the door but faced her. I couldn't take my eyes off of her, she really was something. I was right about one thing I said earlier, Jake was a fucking idiot to cheat on her.

After a few moments, I couldn't control what was about to happen. Something just took over my body. I ran my thumb across my bottom lip and patted the seat next to me, so she would move closer. She was nervous, her body language gave her away. Even if she was trying to hide it, she couldn't. She scooted across, so she was close to me, her breathing sped up.

I placed my hand on her leg, like I did on the way to the restaurant. I could see the reaction that one, single gesture could do. I moved my other hand slowly up to her face, tucking a loose curl behind her ear.

Her breath caught. I wanted to stop, I didn't want to go down this road with her, but I couldn't stop.

She was like a drug that I craved, a drug that I had never tasted before. But I wanted to taste her. So fucking bad. I ran my hand softly down her face, along her cheek bone then slowly run my thumb across her plump bottom lip.

"I want to kiss you," I whispered to her.

"Kiss me then," she whispered back.

I didn't need to hear anymore. I cupped my hand around the back of her head and pulled her towards me. My lips touched hers as I softly kissed her. My heart raced, I felt like fire was burning through my body. I was being taken over by her, I felt like I was already addicted to her by that one, sweet taste.

I moved my hand that was firmly on her thigh as I traced it slowly down and run it across the hem of her dress. It took everything in me to stop myself. I just wanted to push her dress up and expose and explore every inch of her.

My kiss got deeper, my tongue exploring her mouth, I kept my kiss slow and tender, I didn't want to make it fierce. I slowly trailed my hand up her dress before she pulled away, catching her breath. I was taken aback.

"Slowly, take it slow," she whispered to me, steadying her fast breath as she knotted her fingers together. She mumbled, "Sorry." Oh baby, don't be sorry.

I cupped her chin and tilted her face to look at me. "Don't say sorry, I've wanted to do that from the moment I stepped into your office. Do you know how many times I have had to stop myself coming over to your office this week and making a move on you?" I said, my pulse racing. I couldn't work out what was a lie, and what was the truth anymore. I was head fucked. I had lost my head, and it was all because of her.

"You are a wonderful woman, Freya, a woman I want to get to know better. Please come back for a drink," I asked her again, just wanting to confirm that she still wanted to.

After what felt like hours of waiting, she spoke. "I shouldn't, because I know what will happen, I will come back... we will have a drink and then..." She looked up at me.

"And then what?" I asked.

"And then we would end up sleeping together and then that would make work awkward as you wouldn't want to know me anymore."

Oh darling Freya. You poor, poor girl. She really has no

confidence whatsoever. I watched as she faced and looked out the window, obviously embarrassed by what she had just said. I exhaled deeply.

"Why would you think that? I like you Freya."

She placed her hand on mine. "One step at a time, Carter."

I leant over and kissed her on the forehead. "Okay, if that's what you want," I muttered.

I couldn't force her into it. I couldn't take advantage of her. I could with anyone else, but it felt wrong with her.

Before I knew it, we were outside her apartment block. James left the car to open the door for Freya to get out. I knew I wasn't going in hers, but I had to get out and see her to her door

"Honestly, stay in the car, I'll be okay," she said before turning to James. "Thank you." He nodded politely and smiled at her before getting back into the car. I ignored her, obviously.

As she walked up the stairs, I followed close behind her. "Let me at least see you into your apartment?" I didn't like her in this shithole. She just nodded back at me, not saying another word.

We walked up the stairs in silence as she fished around for her keys then opened her door.

"Thank you, Carter for a wonderful night," she said. I stepped forward and placed my hand on her hip.

"You are most welcome, Freya, sleep tight." I leant in

and have her a soft kiss goodnight. I didn't want to leave her, but I had to. I had already got waylaid tonight, and I needed to stick back to my plan.

"Goodnight, Carter," she said before walking into her apartment.

I turned and walked down the stairs. I knew she was watching me but I daren't look back as I wouldn't be able to leave. I walked out of the apartment block and straight into my waiting car. I didn't say anything to James, I just sat in the car throwing my head back against the headrest. James pulled away and started our journey home when all of a sudden, an urge coursed through me. I couldn't go. I needed to go back. Just the once. She wanted me as much as I wanted her.

This one night would be off the plan, I needed her to be mine. If only for one night.

"James," I barked. "Turn the car around, take me back to Freya's," I demanded.

"Of course, Mr. Cole, doing it now," he replied.

I let out a sigh. I couldn't wait to get back to her.

I'm not leaving until I brand her and make her mine completely.

CHAPTER THIRTEEN

Within minutes we were back outside her apartment block. I took a deep breath, I felt so nervous. I sat in the car for five minutes trying to calm my breathing and collect my thoughts before barging in there. I grabbed my phone and left the car.

"James, go home. I will call you in the morning," I said before leaving the car. I slammed the door behind me and jogged up the steps to the communal door, pulling it open and running up the stairs to her front door.

I stopped and counted to three. "One... Two... Three."

I undone my suit jacket and knocked on the door. The front door swung open, my heart stopped beating. My throat dry and tight. Her facial expression mirrored mine. Oh shit.

She stood there in front of me, her big grey eyes burning into my mine. She looked so hot in her oversized guns 'n' roses tee, her beautiful auburn hair pulled into a messy bun with bits escaping and cascading down her face.

"Carter wh——" she said, but I stopped her. I didn't want to talk. I picked her up, holding her tight as she wrapped her legs around my waist, our mouths finding each other.

I melted as she wrapped her arms around my neck, pulling on the nape of my neck before her hands moved to explore my hair, tugging and pulling as our kiss got deeper and more fierce.

I finally slammed the door shut and carried her into the living room. I broke my kiss to explore the inside of her little flat, it was a shit tip. I was laughing inside as I could see the mortified look on her face.

"Please, don't look it's a mess." She blushed. I couldn't give a toss about the house, I just wanted my lips back on hers. I smiled at her before pushing my lips back on hers, losing ourselves. I sat down on the sofa, pulling her down on top of me. I didn't release my grip on her, and she pushed her hands round to my face then ran her fingers along my jaw line.

I moved my hands from her waist and trailed them under her T-shirt, wrapping my fingers around her hips. I moved my lips from her lips, tracing kisses down to her neck. Her head rolled back slightly as she let her self be consumed by just my touch.

Just as I was getting into the flow, she whispered, "Stop."

She sat straddled over me, trying to catch her breath. I

looked up at her beautiful face, my eyes burning with desire and hunger.

"Why did you come back?" she asked. I sat back, keeping my eyes on her the whole time.

"I didn't want to go home without you." It wasn't a lie. I didn't want to go home without her. I moved closer to her, my breath on her. She bit her lip which drove me wild, I just wanted to sink my teeth into it and pull it between my teeth.

"I'm not very good at this, you know, so..." she said looking down. I placed my index finger on her lips to silence her.

"I don't believe you," I said hushed. She reached up and moved my finger from her lips and dropped my hand into her lap.

"Why do you think my ex cheated on me?" she asked. I looked at her, seriously, no expression on my face.

"Because he is an idiot," I said bluntly.

She shook her head. "I've never slept with anyone else, we didn't really do this... it was scheduled for certain nights and certain times," she said.

What the fuck has he done to this poor girl. He has completely shattered her and ruined her confidence. I wanted to make her forget about him, about all the previous times and just focus on giving her me.

I smirked up at her while slowly lifting her T-shirt up, a stupid grin pulled at the side of my lips when I saw her white, lacy thong.

"He's even more of an idiot now," I said, my voice husky. Her body was immense, I could imagine what it was like when she was clothed but nothing could prepare me for what was actually under her clothes. She was phenomenal.

My lips pressed back onto her neck as I planted her with soft, wet kisses, moving slowly down to her collar bone while my hands started to explore her. I moved my hand down around her bum, savouring every touch and sensation that was pulsing through me.

I was growing so hard, I had to stop myself just lifting her off of me and fucking her. I wanted to enjoy every second and show her what a real man feels like. I moved my hand from her bum and trailed my fingers in between her thighs, slowly caressing her through her lacy material.

Her breathing got deeper and faster, small whimpers leaving her lips as the pleasure started rippling through her. I continued with this slow rhythm that I was putting her through, I could tell she was building for an orgasm. Her breathing changed, her face and chest flushed.

I kept my eyes on her, before covering her mouth with mine. My tongue intruding hers, animating the rhythm of my fingers. I pulled away as I wrapped my fingers around her delicate panties, pulling them to the side exposing her.

My mouth went dry, her perfectly waxed apex enticing me. I was so turned on by her. I moved my fingers back to their place, finding her opening and sliding my finger deep inside of her, pushing deeper on each thrust. She laid back slightly as I continued pushing deep inside her, she was so wet for me and tight.

A low 'mmm' escaped me as I felt her tighten around me. "You feel so good," I muttered as I continued to bring her closer to her ecstasy.

She was lost in me, her hips moving with me as I carried on slowly teasing her with my fingers, slowly pushing in and out.

I leant closer to her ear and whispered, "You are driving me wild, I can't wait to fuck you."

She gasped as the crude words left my lips. I slowly pulled my fingers from her, covering her back over with her knickers. I heard the small whimper as the loss of contact from me. I lifted her off me and went over to where I threw my jacket, grabbing a condom out of my pocket.

"Come" I said softly, holding my hand out for her. She stepped slowly, taking my hand and letting me lead her to her bedroom. I cleared the bed of her clothes and stood close to her at the foot of the bed, staring down at her. Not wanting this moment to end. She leant up and kissed me, my hands resting on her hips. She slowly ran her hands down my chest and started undoing my shirt buttons.

I don't normally let people undress me, it's never normally this intimate. I was curious as she took a step back, obviously admiring the view of my torso. I stood there, letting her drink me in. She stepped closer, running her finger from my chest down to my snail trail and along the belt of my suit trousers.

I knew where she was taking this. No chance. This was about her.

I shook my head at her, I picked her up and laid her on the bed beneath me.

"Tonight's about you," I said quietly, smiling down at her.

I took a moment to just admire the stunning view beneath me. I pushed her legs apart and smirked, moving up towards her and kissing her softly again. My heart was thumping so fast. I ran my hand back down her body until I reached the apex of her thighs and run my fingers harshly across her sweet spot.

I unbuckled my belt and kicked my trousers off, then pushed my boxers down my legs and kicked them away. She rested herself up on her elbows, smirking as she took in all of me. I slid the rubber down my cock before kneeling in between her legs and lifting her tee above her head and tossing it to the side of the bed.

"I like your underwear, Freya. It seems a shame to remove it," I said quietly. She blushed a crimson at my words. I loved how she reacted.

I unclipped her bra and pushed the straps slowly down her arms, taking in every moment. Once I had discarded of the bra, I made my way to her panties, sliding them down her luscious, long legs and taking them off of her feet. I moved myself between her legs and slowly inserted a finger back inside of her, slowly stretching her so she was ready for me. The last thing I wanted to do was hurt her. I wanted to take my time with her, I wanted to remember everything from tonight. She was so ready for me.

"Are you ready?" I asked her, and she nodded nervously.

Oh, baby, please don't be nervous I said to myself.

I removed my finger from her before slowly pushing myself into her. Fuck me, she felt so good around me. She gasped as I pushed as far as I could into her, gently and slowly so she could get used to me. I continued the slow movements, not wanting to ruin this for her.

I watched her the whole time, her face over taken by the pleasure I was giving her. I could feel every inch of her, tightly clasped around me. I had to stop myself from exploding, I have never felt anything like her.

She flicked her stunning eyes up to me, connecting our souls in that one moment. Something inside me clicked as she took over my body and soul. Once I knew she was okay, I picked up the pace, moving faster and harder inside of her.

I took one of her breasts into my mouth, sucking and licking her hard nipple. Moans started to leave her body, she liked it. I continued to do what she liked, I wanted her to crumble around me. She lifted her head slightly, watching as I moved in and out of her, her tightening around me again, she was getting close to her orgasm.

"Carter," she moaned in a whisper. I couldn't help but

look at her and smirk. "I'm going to come," she said in a quiet, heavenly cry.

I started ploughing into her faster. I was so close, and I wanted to come with her, share our first orgasm together. With one final thrust her back arched, my hand holding her hip, taking her weight as she arched off of the bed as her orgasm hit her body hard. I followed her, crashing down hard inside of her. I was completely intoxicated.

I rolled off of her and laid next to her, trying to catch my breath.

What the fuck was that?

That wasn't a fuck. That was making love. I tried to slow my thoughts, my heart ached, my body coming alight as I stared at her, beautiful her.

"You were amazing," I said, leaning up on my side, kissing her gently. I smirked when she pulled her duvet up to her face to try and hide. "Hey, don't hide," I said as I pulled the duvet away from her face and looked down at her.

"I'm going to the bathroom," she whispered. I marvelled at her as she sat up, her eyes hunting around the room for her T-shirt. She found it and slipped it over her head before making away to her bathroom.

I laid for a moment as these alien feelings swam through me. I'm just sex drunk. I'll be okay once I'm home. I can't stay here, I've got to go.

My brain was telling my body to move, but it wouldn't. I took a few moments to just catch my breath, pushing everything to the back of my mind. Before I could stop it, I felt the room start to go black around me. It was too late, the exhaustion of the last few nights had hit me, and I was gone.

I was in big trouble; this girl has hooked me. I can't not be near her. I had no control; my heart had found the one and I couldn't tell it otherwise.

CHAPTER FOURTEEN

I woke with a jolt. It took me a while to realise where I was and who was next to me. I pulled my arm away quickly before sitting up and looking round the room. I was still at Freya's. I didn't even remember falling asleep. I had obviously been cuddling her in the night, as much as it seemed to thaw my icy heart, it didn't feel natural.

I checked my phone, squinting when the bright light reflected in my eyes. I groaned, it was six-thirty am. Damn body clock. I sneaked out of bed, I needed to piss so bad. I tiptoed through to her bathroom closing the door quietly.

As I was washing my hands, I studied my face in her mirror. My eyes sparkled, they didn't seem dull anymore. I splashed my face with cold water, I needed to snap out of this little fantasy I was living in.

I tiptoed out the bathroom and into the kitchen, popping the kettle on. I rummaged through her cupboards. I was hungry, but I didn't know what I wanted. I sighed as I shut the door, I walked over to her small living area and flopped down on the sofa, sitting, staring round the room.

She had piles of magazines, a bookshelf full of books, photos dotted all around her room. I sat forward and focused on one of the pictures. There was Freya and two other ladies, one blonde, one brunette. I wondered who they were. I shrugged it off as I sat quietly for a moment or two. I just wanted to try and quiet my mind from the constant thoughts about what the fuck I had gotten myself into, and how the bloody hell was I going to get out of it, but I didn't know if I wanted to get out of it.

This was my problem. I wanted her but didn't want her at the same time.

I moved from the sofa back into the kitchen area and made myself and her a cup of tea. It had just gone seven when I heard footsteps coming towards me.

I bought my cup to my lips and took a mouthful as I saw her walk in the room. I trailed my eyes up and down her, stopping at her eyes.

How could someone make an oversized tee and her hair scraped on her head look stunning? She really was something else. I had never felt so conflicted in my life.

My head was telling to get the fuck out, go back to my life but my heart was begging me to stay, to drop my guard and go full pelt into a relationship with her and never let her go. I hadn't even known her that long, yet I felt like I had known her a lifetime.

"Hey, you," she said shyly as she leant towards the

doorframe to her bedroom. God, I wanted to take her back into that room and devour every inch of her. I turned for a moment just to breathe before turning back round to her.

"Good morning, how did you sleep? Sugar?" I stood holding the teaspoon waiting for her answer.

"I slept very well, Mr Cole, what about you? And no, thank you." She smiled as she walked over towards me, slowly. I handed her the cup before kissing her softly on her lips.

"Best sleep I've had in ages." I beamed at her. It wasn't a lie, I can't remember the last time I slept that deeply.

"Okay to jump in the shower?" I asked as I walked towards the bedroom, her eyes following me from over her shoulder while nodding. I slipped into her bathroom, locking the door before standing under her shitty shower.

The pressure was awful, the water was luke-warm. I stepped out and wrapped myself in her stiff towel before looking through her bathroom cabinet and grabbing the mouthwash. I dried myself off before wrapping the towel back round me as I made my way back into her bedroom.

I looked around the room for my clothes when I noticed Freya pointing over to her chest of drawers.

"Thank you," I muttered.

"I'm going to get in the shower, I need to be with Laura for ten thirty, the train journey is going to take forty-five minutes," she said to me. I tucked my inside out pockets of my suit trousers as I walked over to her.

"I will drive you," I said.

"Oh, so you do drive then?" she said with a silly smirk on her face.

"Yes, Freya, I do drive," I said slightly aggravated.

"Okay, well I'm going to jump in shower and get ready, I won't be long. There's bread in the cupboard or cereal, help yourself," she said before slipping into the bathroom.

I eyed up that her clothes were laid out on the bed. I smirked to myself, another chance of seeing her. I threw my crinkled white shirt on and sat on her bed. I grabbed my phone off her bedside table and had a look through my emails and rolled my eyes at the amount that were unread.

I rubbed my temples. I felt like I needed a break from work. Ten minutes had passed, and my eyes flicked up when I felt eyes on me. Freya stood in the doorway with her towel wrapped round her, her cascading curls swept over her shoulder. We didn't say anything, I just followed her with my eyes.

She grabbed a silk pair of panties and went to slide them up her legs still with her towel wrapped round her. I stood and moved towards her, shaking my head and I stepped in front of her, dropping her towel to the floor.

"I want to look at you, it was dark last night so I didn't get to enjoy the view."

She blushed a crimson red.

"Freya, don't be embarrassed, you have a very sexy body."

I loved that I towered over her, looking down at her before placing my hands round her waist.

"You should come to work like this. I could look at you all day, but then I don't know how much work we would get done," I teased. I laughed as she laughed out loud at my comment.

"I don't think Jools would be very happy." I clocked my head.

"When is she ever happy?" I asked.

"That's true," she chirped. I leaned in and kissed her. I could kiss her all day if she would let me. I whined inside as she peeled my arms from around her.

"I really need to get ready, you don't know Laura. She can't stand when people are late, and apparently, I am always late," she huffed before slipping into her silk panties. *Fuck, she looked incredible.* Why couldn't we just stay here and fuck?

I watched her constantly, watching her potter around her room making herself up, not that she needed to, but she really was breath taking. She picked her phone up and started tapping on the phone screen, smiling sweetly as she read her message as she wrote.

She sprayed her perfume, Chanel No. 5 by the looks of it. Ah, that's why it smelt familiar. She pulled me from my daydream.

"Come on, handsome, we've got to go," she said as she started walking down her hallway to the front door.

"Right behind you, baby," I said as I walked behind her, then heading to the front door as she stopped to pick her bag up. *Baby?* I don't think I have ever called one of my girls' 'baby'. But that was the issue, she wasn't 'one of my girls,' and I don't think I want her to be.

I opened the door and waited out on the communal landing as she stepped out and locked the front door. We walked down the communal stairs together, hand in hand when I felt her grip loosen which only made me grasp her hand tighter.

I couldn't work out why she was trying to pull her hand from mine, then I saw him. This blonde-haired fucker down at the communal letterboxes. I looked at her, sheer panic all over her face.

"Hey Freya." He beamed at her. I tightened my grip around her hand, so she couldn't walk away from me.

"Hey Ethan!" she said a little too enthusiastic. "How are you? Did you have a nice night?" she asked him, his eyes on her the whole time.

Who the fuck was this surf dude wanna be and what did he want with Freya?

"Yea, I'm fine, it was good, take it yours went well then?" he asked her. She tried to pull her hand from mine again, but I wasn't going to let her go. She looked up at me, I couldn't read her face which annoyed me then I focused my eyes on Ethan while she still gawked at me.

"Erm, yea, it did," she mumbled uncomfortably.

"Good," he replied bluntly to her response.

I couldn't help but puff my chest out a bit more knowing how put out he was that I had spent the night with her. They stood in an awkward silence for a moment or two before Freya spoke.

"Anyway, I've got to run, bridesmaid dress fitting."

I was still staring at Ethan, Ethan staring at me. I wanted to punch him right here right now and knock him the fuck out. Then he smirked before saying, "Yeah cool, will text you later," before walking towards his shitty apartment.

I watched as Freya clearly relaxed. We made our way outside to my grey Maserati sitting kerbside. Thank god James was up early to bring it over. I was feeling pissed. I opened Freya's car door, not looking or saying a word to her. Something has happened between Ethan and her and I want to know what the fuck it was. I shut her door before making my way to my side and slamming the door behind me, wanting to let her know I was pissed off.

"What is wrong with you?" she asked, confusion on her face, her eyes squinting slightly at me.

I huffed and plugged myself in before answering. "Nothing. I just didn't like the way he was looking at you, like you were his property or something," I said, my eyes focused on the roads.

She scoffed at my comment. Oh, was I about to meet feisty Freya?

"I am no one's property. Ethan is a friend, a good

friend."

Oh you are mistaken, Miss Greene.

You are my property, I have branded you. I won't let you go. I tightened my grip on the steering wheel as I asked the next question.

"Do you like him like that?" Not sure if I really wanted to know the answer.

"I do like him, yes." I saw her mutter something under her breath after saying that, and I chose to ignore it.

"Have you been on a date with him?" I asked her another question that I knew would annoy her, and it did.

She rolled her eyes at me. "Yes, we went for drinks after work last week. He's new to the building and area."

I frowned at the thought that she had been on a date with him. I didn't want her going on a date with him, or anyone for the matter. We pulled up in traffic as I pulled my eyes from the road and focused on her.

"I don't want you seeing anyone else," I snapped.

"Are you joking?" she stammered back at me. My eyes focused back on the road as I responded.

"No, Freya. I am not joking. I don't want anyone else near you apart from me," I said coolly, wanting her to know that this is how I wanted it.

"Pull over, I want to get out," she snapped, clearly pissed off with me.

"What?" I asked like an idiot.

"You heard me, pull over. I am not having you telling

me what to do. In work I have to listen to you, you are technically my boss, but out of work I don't have to, so pull over," she said angrily, her brows furrowed, her words like venom.

I pulled over to the kerb like she asked. I couldn't argue with her, I didn't want to argue with her. But I did say quietly, "Freya, please don't do this," as she opened the door.

"I didn't do anything, Carter, you did!" she said in a raised tone, slamming the door then moving onto the pavement.

I stopped the car, looking down into my lap, embarrassed to look back at her and also, embarrassed with my behaviour. I am never like this, why is she getting into my head? She just stood there, as if she was waiting for me to say something. I was going to make her late, and I didn't want her waiting for a taxi, or worse, calling Ethan. It's like she read my mind and decided to get back into the car. I took her right hand, running my thumb across the back of her knuckles.

"Freya, I'm sorry. I just get protective because I like you," I say before planting a soft kiss on the back of her hand. She didn't say anything to me, just looked out the window as I pulled away from the kerb.

Oh man, I've fucked up.

I looked over at her, her big sun glasses covering her eyes as she stayed looking forward. The silence in the car was too much, so I put Luther Vandross on which helped the rest of the painfully, silent journey.

CHAPTER FIFTEEN

We pulled up outside the bridal shop, minutes before Freya's appointment. We still hadn't spoken, and it was killing me. She opened her car door and slipped out, before she walked away I opened my window and bent my head down.

"I'm sorry, baby," I grovelled. She leant down, her glasses pushed on top of her head as she smirked at me.

"Thank you for the lift, loved Luther by the way," she said before turning on her heel and walking into the bridal shop. Oh touché Miss Greene. Little minx. I was annoyed at how I reacted, but I didn't like the way he literally drooled over her.

I wanted to get home, Louis still hadn't called me back, the prick. I needed to talk to someone, anyone. I floored the car most of the way home until I pulled into the penthouse carpark, slamming the door as I left.

I sulked my way into my lift and tapped my fingers impatiently on the steel handrail. I sighed in relief when the doors pinged opened.

"Julia!" I shouted out, searching the kitchen and the hallway. I rolled my eyes when she didn't respond. Just when I was about to call my mum, I saw James walking round the corner and into the kitchen.

"James!" I called out. I felt like I was pacing around, panicked, looking for someone to pour my heart out too.

"Hey, Carter, all okay boss?" he asked as he poured a glass of tap water. "Want one?" he saidI shook my head at him.

"No, no thanks." I kept my eyes on him, counting to five in my head before talking again. "Are you free for a chat?" I asked him, not wanting to keep him from his job.

"Of course, everything okay?" he asked as he sat on the stool under the breakfast bar, his eyes boring into mine.

"I don't know. I am so confused, and I have no one to talk to about it." I huffed. James just blew his cheeks out and widened his eyes.

"Man, what's happened to you?" James then laughed while he waited for my response.

"This girl is getting into my fucking head. I literally went on one date, fucked her and now I am obsessed with her. I don't want anyone going near her, I don't want to go near anyone but her! I feel like calling up the girls I see and terminating them. Honestly, I just don't know what to do. Then we had a shitty row because we bumped into someone she had a measly date with and it fucked me off even more knowing that he has taken her out and potentially touched her, even though she said she hadn't done anything with him. It is driving me insane." I groaned as I put my head into my hands, trying to calm the thumping that was going on. I could feel the blood pumping through my veins.

"Woah, okay... that was a lot to take in." James smirked, twirling his glass round on the worktop. "Shit, Carter, you are in deep," he said still smirking.

"James, I need help mate, not shitty, useless comments," I said, frustrated as I started rubbing my temples.

"Okay, man, I'm sorry. Okay, so you like her then?" he asked the stupid question and I rolled my eyes at him.

"Yes. I do like her, but I don't know what to do. Do I pursue it or cut my ties with her?" I hit my fist on the table. "I only wanted to get her to fall for me, so I could then destroy her, so I could get back with Aimee, but the truth is, Aimee has nothing on her." I sighed.

"She does seem lovely. I know I've only met her a few times but there is just something about her," he said to me.

"Alright, mate, do you want to sleep with her too?!" I said a little louder than I intended to, then sighing, "See what I mean, look what she is doing to me!"

"No! of course not, I'm bloody married to Julia, you idiot." He laughed. "Man, she has done a number on you," he said chuckling before drinking his water.

"I wanna see her. Maybe I should mention about her

being one of my flavours, what do you think? Maybe test the water, see if she is up for it?" I asked him.

"Well, why don't you then? You might be able to gauge her a bit more then. I can't see her wanting to do it, then that way you can leave the whole 'revenge' plan and just try to pursue Aimee another way, if that's still what you want." He shrugged as he stood up.

"Okay, I will. I'll text her, need to apologise for being a dick anyway so makes sense." I nodded. "Thanks, James, sorry to burden you with this but I have no one else to talk to." I smiled a little at him.

"No worries, Carter, always here if you want a chat," he said before leaving the kitchen and disappearing.

I stalked up to my en-suite and peeled my clothes off my sticky body. I felt dirty. I moved under the shower, letting the water take over my body, trying to think about what I was going to say to her. I wrapped my towel around me and flopped onto the bed, picking my phone as I did, having a flick through my emails. I groaned at the ever-growing list of the unread emails. It was gone one pm when I decided to finally get dressed after being glued to my phone most of the morning while I sorted through my pointless emails.

Why employ staff if they couldn't deal with the easiest of situations? Bellends.

I ran downstairs and grabbed a cup of coffee, sitting in

the silence of this empty penthouse. I was so fucking lonely. I never noticed how bad it was until recently. Maybe I didn't want this anymore? Different girl, different week. I just didn't know what to do for the best, I knew I had to make a decision. Maybe I should do what I said to James, see if she wants to be a 'flavour' then we can go from there. I pulled my phone off charge and typed a quick message to her

Hey, I am really sorry about earlier, come over to my place tonight and I will make it up to you, Carter X

I breathed out the breath I had been holding as I waited for little note underneath to tell me it had been delivered. I would take her to my townhouse, I didn't want to bring her here. I wanted to show her my other home. The home that *if* things did progress further we could maybe live and bring up children in.

My heart fluttered as I thought about it, my head soon brought me back round with vile and bitter thoughts.

What is wrong with you? Settling down with some chick. Didn't your dad teach you anything!? Don't fall in love. Stay an arsehole. An arsehole who can fuck for as long as he wants.

No women holding you down or back. No worry about a wandering eye.

All you have to worry about is you, and only you.

Fucking settling down, get a grip, Cole.

Anger rose in me. I felt so conflicted and I didn't know how much more I could take. I left my phone on the kitchen side and sulked into the gym.

Placing my earphones in my ears, I started taking my anger out on the punch bag, hitting it again and again while grunting out my frustration. I could call my mum to talk about this but then she would only tell me to follow my heart and enjoy the company of someone.

I hated being lonely. I never went out with my friends, I worked and fucked. Sounded like the perfect life, right? But it was a miserable, lonely, heart-breaking life.

Money doesn't buy you happiness, look at me. I am rich beyond my means, I could have any car I wanted, any house I wanted and yet I was still miserable. I hated my life, I hated what I had become.

Maybe Freya was the one to change that. I knew I hardly knew her, but there was something about her that kept me wanting to get to know her. I wanted to explore this life with her. I needed to see how she felt when I saw her tonight, if I saw her tonight.

She was still pretty pissed with me after my comment and the surfer wannabe.

After a few more rounds of punching the shit out of my punch bag, I felt like some tension had lifted. I was dripping with sweat, my heart racing. I slid down the wall as I undid my hands.

I took a few deep breaths to calm my breathing before making my way back upstairs. I poured myself an iced water then checked my phone, still nothing from her. Fuck, she was stubborn. I typed another message.

Freya, please answer me. I will send a car for 7:30, see you soon X

If she doesn't reply in the next ten minutes I am driving over there. Almost instantly my phone vibrated. A wicked smirk across my face spread like wild fire as I saw her name. *Finally.*

See you at 7:30, looking forward to talking x

Was that it? That must be the bluntest message ever, and look forward to talking?? Oh man, maybe she has some stuff that she wants to talk about? I walked over to the living area and threw myself on the sofa looking for a movie to lose myself in. *21 Jump Street,* perfect.

-

I sat in the back of the car, my palms sweaty. Running my hands down my black skinny jeans, I was so nervous to see her, and it had only been a few hours.

We got stuck in traffic, putting me behind schedule. I hated being late. I looked at my watched and groaned, it was seven-thirty already and we were still at least ten minutes from Freya's. I didn't want to text her, as I didn't want to come across needy. She knew I would be there, I hadn't cancelled on her.

I sat back and closed my eyes, thinking about how I was going to plan this evening out. I knew I was going to cook for her, then maybe approach her for the chat. The chat that could end this all tonight and get me out of this shit I was in. I didn't want it to end, but I couldn't go through with this revenge. I just couldn't do it. If she didn't want to be one of my flavours, then I had to think about what I wanted to do.

I sighed in relief when we pulled up outside her block, "I'll be five minutes," I said to James as I left the car and made my way into her building.

I stood at the bottom of the stairs that led up to her flat when I could hear muffled voices. I closed my eyes, for some reason I thought that made me be able to listen better.

"I want you to leave," I heard her hushed, abrupt voice.

"Freya, I..." I heard a male's voice. I recognised it, shit that was Ethan's! "I'm sorry, I just, I can't even explain what was going through my head..."

"Ethan, I want you to leave, please," I heard her say again, this time desperation in her voice. I wasn't listening anymore, I ran up the few stairs until I stood in the doorway, staring on, adrenaline pumping through me.

Freya was backed against the wall, Ethan's arm

stopping her from moving. I felt the bile rise in my throat, the anger that started coursing through my veins.

"She told you to leave," I said in a slow, low grunt of a voice. My eyes glazed over and hooded as I kept my eyes on the fuck-wit the whole time. I wanted to smash his face in, but I couldn't do that, I couldn't do that to her.

"I'm sorry," he mumbled pathetically to her as he rushed passed me and down to his flat. I ran to her side.

"Are you okay?" I whispered as I stroked the back of my hand across her cheek bone.

"I'm fine, he just wanted to talk about earlier, and he was upset," she said quietly. I didn't want to push it, she was clearly shaken up and still pissed with me. I didn't want to start our evening on an argument, so I just nodded.

"Come on, lock up. The cars outside," I said before pressing my lips to her forehead, a familiar buzz trickling through me from my head to my toes. I took her hand firmly and led her downstairs to James, she flashed her perfect smile at him.

"Evening, James," she said before getting into the car. I finally got to look at her, her hair straightened, her face glowing. She had this tiny white T-shirt dress on that was slightly see through. I could see her underwear underneath. I would have made a comment but didn't want to embarrass her, just in case she didn't realise.

"You look wonderful, Freya," I said softly, my eyes alight and glistening. I see her blush.

"What in this old thing?" She giggled, which made me laugh at her. "You don't look too bad yourself," she swooned.

We didn't say anymore, just sat in silence looking out at beautiful London. I'm not sure if it was out of awkwardness, or whether it was just that we were comfortable enough with each other. I fidgeted in my seat for a moment, before bending down and pulling a box out from under my seat.

"This is a little gift for you, a sorry present for being a jerk," I said, shrugging as I handed her the big brown Louis Vuitton box. She looked up at me like a deer in headlights.

"I can't accept this, Carter, it's too much," she said, barely saying the words. I clasped her hands in mine.

"Please, Freya, it's a gift." I smiled at her as her eyes moved back to the box.

I watched as she ran her fingertips along the edging, tracing every detail. She finally lifted the lid off of the box, and her face lit up. Her eyes glistening, her mouth opened slightly in shock. She placed the box on the floor before throwing herself onto me, wrapping her arms around my neck then kissing me sweetly on the lips.

"Thank you, Carter, but you really didn't have to. Let me pay you back, I can't accept this as a gift," she said, her arms still tightly round my neck. It was silent for a few moments before I snaked my arms around her waist, pulling her into my lap.

"Call it a bonus," I teased before winking at her. I watched her frown.

"Please let me pay you back."

Man, she wasn't going to drop this.

"I'll think about it." I smirked at her, there is no way she is paying me back, plus this is a little sweetener of what she could be getting from me. She shook her head in disagreement.

"Please," she whispered to me again, and I stared at her.

"I said I would think about it," I reply, saying it with enough of a clip in my voice for her to get it, but not before kissing her forehead again. Her scent intoxicating me.

"You smell good," I mumbled to her. She moved towards me, kissing me again, this time she lingered that bit longer, a few soft tongue strokes before I pulled away. "As much as I want to stay kissing you, we are here, and I've got to cook us dinner."

I could see the confused look on her face as she eyed the townhouse. I knew she expected that we would go to the penthouse, but I wanted to surprise her.

"Welcome to Birchwood," I said smiling at her as I lifted her off my lap. I left the car, taking her hand for her to follow me.

CHAPTER SIXTEEN

I watched Freya's jaw hit the floor at the grand entrance hallway. I loved watching her expressions. Half of me wanted to just forget about what I had planned tonight but the other part of me needed to see how she reacted.

This could be my way out. I had already played it out in my head on what I was going to do and say. I had a dinner planned then take her downstairs to the bar and pool area, then tell her and ask her to be one of my flavours. I don't want her to agree, I can't deny that there is a pull between us and I know she feels the same. I couldn't work out what was happening. I wanted her so bad, but I didn't want anyone else to have her. But I'm not sure if I am ready to give this up yet.

I am so used to doing things my way, a particular way shall we say, that I don't know deep down what I want anymore. I was disturbed from my thoughts when she started walking towards the kitchen. She stopped in her tracks, then looked over her shoulder to make sure it was okay. I gave her a gentle nod before she continued towards the kitchen. I stayed silent, walking behind her. I made my way to the wine fridge and grabbed a bottle of white.

"Wine?" I asked.

She replied, "Yes please," as she ran her fingertips along the black, marble worktop as she walked towards me. I poured myself and her a large glass, I needed it and I am sure she did too. I handed her the glass as I took a small sip.

"Here you go."

She smiled as she thankfully took the glass from my grip. A few moments passed of pure silence, my sage eyes on hers the whole time. She broke the silence.

"So, what's for dinner? I am starving."

I smiled at her as I stood by the fridge. "Good, steak okay?" I asked watching as she sat up at the breakfast bar.

"Steak is perfect, medium rare please, chef," she jokingly replied, which made me chuckle. She was so easy to be around. I instantly felt relaxed in her company, I felt like I didn't have to put on a false pretence with her which instantly put me at ease, and I liked it. She caught me off guard with her next question.

"So, what is an almost perfect man like you, doing single?" Her grey eyes watching me move around the kitchen. I turned from the stove to face her, scoffing at her question as I did.

"Almost perfect?" I questioned her with a teasing tone.

She nodded.

"Well, that's what I wanted to talk to you about," I said. I watched as she raised her eyebrows in shock at what I had just said that nearly made her choke on her drink. Maybe she thinks I am going to ask her to be my girlfriend, I laughed to myself. Silly girl.

I could see her eyes darting back and forth to mine, she then cleared her throat, her eyes wide. I felt like I could see into her soul, a soul I could easily lose myself in.

I pulled myself out of my daze as she said quietly, "Oh, did you? What about?" She tried to sound confident, but her voice was shaky, she was nervous.

I threw the tea towel over my shoulder and got our plates out of the hot oven. I let our steaks sit for a moment as I served the fresh asparagus up, then served a big slice of dauphinoise potatoes. I then plated up the perfectly cooked steak. I slid the plate over to her cautiously, then slid mine next to hers, pulling the chilled bottle of wine over to us. I then took my seat next to her before topping both of our wine glasses up.

"Let's eat first," I suggested, trying to reason with her but also trying to keep her mind off of it. I could tell she wasn't happy with that answer, but I wasn't doing it now. I grabbed my phone and put the piano guys on which filled the room subtly.

We started talking about my family, mostly about my mum. I never spoke about my family but talking to Freya was so easy and I felt like she wouldn't judge me. I didn't even know her, yet I couldn't stop my verbal vomit. I finished up by telling her that my mum was coming to stay for the weekend.

I slid off the stool, kissing her on her cheek as I did.

"Did you enjoy that?" I asked, eager to please her for whatever reason.

She nodded. "It was really good, I didn't realise how hungry I was." I watched her still as her breathing fastened as I leant over to collect her plate.

"What's wrong?" I asked. She turned in her seat slightly, clearly nervous.

"You make me nervous," she mumbled. I was confused, I don't remember doing anything to make her nervous or uncomfortable.

"I do?" I asked, she nodded.

"I can't read you and that frustrates me. I can't work out what is going on in your head. I'm normally good at gauging people, but you, you don't let on to anything," she said. I watched as her brow furrowed.

"You don't want to know what's going through my head at the moment," I replied, giving her a half smile. "Come with me, I want to talk to you," I said.

She slid off her stool and adjusted her T-shirt dress as discreetly as she could. My eyes burned into her.

"You don't have to pull that down for my sake, you should be pulling it up," I teased then smirked as she let out a gasp. "You know you would like that," I mumbled.

I took her hand and walked her back into the hallway, through to the back of the living room with a staircase that took us to the basement. I led her to the seating area near the swimming pool, then gestured for her to sit down. I could tell she was nervous, I didn't want her to be nervous.

"Please don't be nervous," I said quietly, putting both of my hands on her knees as I sat down opposite her. "I have something to ask you," I said. I felt nervous now, my heart beating through my chest, and I am sure she could see it. I took a deep breath but done it so she couldn't tell. "Will you be my number seven?"

Her eyes went wide then squinted, focusing on my sage eyes. Shit, this isn't the face I wanted to see from her.

"Your number what?" she said quietly as she shook her head, the confusion painted all over her face. Shit. I sat up in my seat, pressing my index fingers into my chin while resting my elbows on my knees.

"Look, let me explain," I said, taking another deep breath, this time letting her see. She didn't say anything, she just sat there, wide eyed with no doubt a million questions running through her head.

"I have flavours of the month shall we say, seven girls who I alternate between, the next two months will be you. I don't see any of the other girls, you don't see anyone else. Once our two months are up, you go back to your day to day life and once your cycle comes around again, I will call you. You will be paid generously in a wage and gifts."

Her face said a thousand words, I could see as she pushed her hand through her hair in frustration.

"Let me see if I understand you properly," she said abruptly. She stood up and looked down at me, I saw a flicker in her eyes, a flicker that I could see her changing her mind. She wanted me, I wanted her. So bad.

"You want me to be a booty call, for a couple of months, until you are bored of me? I'm not some fucking whore, Carter, you can't just call me up when you want me and pay me in expensive gifts and cash. Is that what the bag was for? A sweetener, a little taster of what I could be getting?"

I needed to calm her down. I stood up and towered over her, my eyes on hers.

"No, the bag was a genuine gift, I'm sure I could get you to change your mind." I ran my hands down the side of her body and stopped at the bottom of her T-shirt dress and hitched it up slightly.

My eyes alight when I hear her breath catch. I took a step closer to her, our lips so close but I stopped myself. I slid my hands higher up her body then ran them back down slowly, running my fingers along her knicker line and along her bum. She pushed my hands away.

"I don't think so. Call James, I want to go home," she mumbled, still standing a bit too close for someone who apparently wants to go home.

"Do you, Freya?" I asked, and within a few seconds of her eyes darting back and forth from mine she replied yes. I reached into my pocket and pulled out my phone and clicked James' name.

"James, please come to Birchwood, Miss Greene wishes to go home."

"Really?" he said.

"Yes," I snapped back.

"So, I take it didn't go well with the whole flavours chat?"

"No" I said, exhausted with his questions.

"Okay, when do you want me to come?"

"Now." I sighed. "Thanks." I cut the phone off.

I threw my phone onto the nest of tables next to the seating area, frustrated with how this conversation went. I wanted her to stay. She threw me when she started talking.

"Can I ask you something?" I didn't say anything, just stayed quiet. "The blonde girl in The Ivy…"

I knew where she was going. I looked at her, I could feel anger building inside of me, but I had to swallow it back down. I needed to keep calm, but it was hard.

"Yes, Freya," I snapped. I watched as she turned back away, staring at the calm pool water.

"Right," she said, staying quiet. I walked up behind her and wrapped my arms round her waist pulling her into me, nuzzling into her neck, smelling her as discreetly as I could. My heart protruding my chest. I slowly moved my hands round to her tummy, her hands finding their way on top of mine.

"What's wrong?" I whispered to her, her eyes meeting mine as she looked over her shoulder.

"Are you winding me up?" she said abruptly, turning around to face me. Her beautiful face stalling me. I can't get over how beautiful she was.

"Why is this such a problem, Freya?" I asked exasperated.

She pulled away from me. "I'm not a booty call, Carter. I actually thought you liked me, but you don't, I'm just a fuck to you," she said with hurt lacing her voice.

I felt frustrated, I grabbed her arm and pulled her back towards me.

"I do like you," I said moving her hand down to my groin area to show her how hard I was for her. "See." I smirked down at her.

"Don't, I'm not interested, Carter. Let's just keep it professional, it's for the best."

The annoying thing was, she was interested. Yet, here she was building her walls up around me. I ran my hand through my messy hair, frustrated.

"I don't want to keep our relationship professional. I want our relationship the way it is. Fun," I said aggravated.

She tilted her head at me, confusion spreading across her face.

"Fun? This isn't fun, this is a booty call. I would be your fuck buddy, friends with benefits – I'm not into that, sorry," she snapped at me.

I was clearly pissed off now and she could tell, her face dropping as soon as she realised she had annoyed me.

"I like to fuck pretty girls, I like to have a selection, so I don't get bored. I like to wine and dine them and show them a good time. You haven't got to worry about having your heart broken, we both get what we want." I tried to persuade her.

She stared stunned at me as if I had just told her I had killed someone. I really didn't get what her issue was with this, it wasn't as if I was asking her to be a sex slave and telling her she was never allowed to leave my sex dungeon ever again.

"That's not what I want," she corrected me. I sulked over to her, my eyes hooded and full of lust.

"Is it not?" I whispered hitching her T-shirt dress up, then dropping to my knees in front of her.

"Carter, get up," she demanded. I ignored her.

I pushed my hands up her soft skin, up her body, pushing her dress higher. I planted soft kisses along her panty-line, slowly moving down to the centre of her panties, pressing my lips harder into her creases as I touched her sweet, delicate spot.

I ran one of my hands back down her body, past her bum then continued to run my fingers under her bum cheek then slowly sliding it at her damp folds. She moaned softly, my fingers continuing their caressing.

I wanted to pull her panties down and enjoy every

piece of her. Her hands found my hair, grabbing a big handful, gently tugging as she started to loosen up. I slipped my fingers inside her panties and inserted one finger slowly, deeply into her, letting out another delicious moan which spurred me on to continue, as I gripped onto the top of her thigh, squeezing it as I did. I looked up at her.

"You don't want this, Freya?"

She kept silent, not muttering a word, intoxicated in me and I fucking loved it. I slipped my finger out of her, then hooked the tips of my fingers in her panties and pulled them down her legs then off her feet.

I was surprised that she didn't stop me. Did she actually want to be one of my girls? I didn't want her to be, but then did. I was so conflicted with what I actually wanted. I shook my thoughts from my mind, placing my hand back on her thigh then covered her with my mouth, my tongue lapping up her taste, she was so wet.

I wanted to consume her, I wanted to keep tasting the sweetness.

Just as I was really losing myself in the moment she started shaking her head.

"Carter, please stop. What about James?" I stopped, whimpering inside with the loss of her taste.

"James knows to wait." I stood up and peeled my T-shirt off. I saw her eyes trailing up and down my body, taking in every inch of me. I kicked my converse off then wrapped my arms around her, kissing her, my tongue invading her innocent mouth. The taste of her still strong on my taste buds. I wanted to continue but I had to stop, I needed to be able to control myself.

"Please consider it," I pleaded.

"I can't be this girl – this isn't me," she said, her eyes wide looking at me.

I let go of her and stepped away. "It's not like I'm asking you to be my submissive, I'm not a dominant, I just want you to myself, to just fuck and have a good time," I said quietly.

She sighed. "I know you're not, but you're basically asking me to be a prostitute."

I was done, I was exhausted with this conversation

"Fine," I snapped. "If that's what you think. Let's go, James is waiting for you."

I picked my T-shirt up, put it back on and slipped into my converse. We walked in silence to the main hall. I was embarrassed, frustrated and full of sexual tension. Normally I would just call one of my girls, but I didn't want too. I wanted her and only her.

I walked her out to James, James smiling at her as he opened the back-passenger door for her.

"Evening, Freya," he said politely. I stood on the pavement with my hands in my pockets, I felt like my eyes were burning into hers, staring at her.

"Bye, Carter," she said, clearly not wanting to say goodbye. I could hear the tightness in her voice where the lump was deep in her throat. She didn't want this. So why was she being so fucking stubborn?

James cut our eye contact as he shut the door, pulling me from my thoughts. I could see her put her head in her hands through the slightly tinted windows. She then threw her head back as she cried. I couldn't let her go. I couldn't leave her crying. Just as James was about to leave I swung the back-door open. Oh my poor Freya.

"Baby, why are you crying? Please don't cry." I knew why she was crying, I couldn't stop the stupid question flying off my tongue. I put my arm around her and pulled her close to me, her head snuggling into me. Neither of us spoke. Nothing needed to be said, too much had been said already tonight.

We pulled up outside Freya's shitty apartment. She pushed off of me and slipped out the car quickly as James opened her door for her, she started running up her stairs.

"Freya, please. Don't leave it like this." Even now I felt choked. I let my eyes glaze over, not wanting her to see the vulnerability in me.

"I can't do it," she said as she faced me, tears filling her eyes, stammering over her words. What the fuck have I done. I have broken this perfect angel. This perfect angel's heart I've torn out of her and destroyed it. I grabbed her hand in a desperate plea to feel that electricity course through me, but there was nothing. I didn't understand.

"Let me go, please," she begged, her eyes on the floor. I didn't want to let her go, I wanted to scream for her to forgive me, but I couldn't. My brain and mouth weren't working. I did as she asked, I reluctantly let go of her hand.

"Bye," she mumbled as she walked through the community door, making her way up the stairs. I saw her look behind, seeing me still standing there, regretting this whole fucking evening and this stupid plan.

Once she was out of sight, I threw my hands over my eyes and tilted my head back, and as if I were in a movie, the rain fell down around me. It was like the heavens were crying over me.

And just like that, the wound of Rylie opened up again. But this time I was afraid I wouldn't be able to close it.

CHAPTER SEVENTEEN

I sat in the back of James' car, soaking wet, not saying anything. I didn't want to say anything. James was dying to ask me where it went wrong, but I couldn't answer. I didn't want to talk about it.

I sat and stared out the window at the realisation of how I fucked it up. Of how I desperately just wanted Freya in my life. No other girls. Just me and her. I thought she would be putty in my hands, I thought she would want this lifestyle, just to be with me. But she didn't. Who could blame her? Her heart was broken by Jake, and I feel like I have just done it to her again.

It was in that moment that I realised I didn't want Aimee, I didn't want to try and get back with her. She was a good fuck, something I thought I wanted, but I don't. She was never interested in me, she only liked the lifestyle that I gave her. I want Freya. In every fucking form.

I sighed with relief when we pulled into the

underground garage of the penthouse. I exited the car quickly before I got collared by James, running for the lift to get me in my safe place. My chest was heaving by the time I was locked behind the lift doors, trying to take a moment to calm my breathing. As the lift doors pinged open, I made my way straight for my shower.

I laid on my bed contemplating my options on how to tell Freya about the 'revenge plan' but nothing seemed right. Everything made me sound like an absolute arsehole, which to be honest, was true. I was an arsehole.

I couldn't do it, I couldn't see this revenge plan out. I didn't want to break her even more than I already had. I had already fallen so hard for her and I barely knew her, yet I knew I wanted her, and only her.

I pulled myself away from the constant back and forth of my thoughts in my head and made my way to my kitchen, grabbing a crystal tumbler before padding over to my drinks cabinet and taking the crystal decanter that was filled with my favourite amber poison out.

I poured myself a generous portion before sitting on my sofa and watching the city come to life beneath me. It was gone three by the time I decided to call it a night and crash into bed, my head feeling heavy and fuzzy as the whiskey soaked through me, helping calm my thoughts slightly.

I let out a deep sigh before falling face down on the bed

and slipping into a deep slumber before I could even think about it.

I woke groggy and pissed off. Pissed off with how things were left with Freya last night, pissed off with letting myself fall so fucking hard already.

This wasn't part of the plan.

This wasn't supposed to happen.

Yes, I wanted to scare Freya off, but yet I still wanted her. I don't even know what to do to get myself out of this.

I moped to the bathroom, splashing my face with cold water and brushing my teeth. The whiskey was still laced on my breath and the taste was making me heave.

I made my way downstairs, looking for James. I needed to talk to him. I was greeted by Julia making breakfast and my stomach growled. I was starving.

"Morning, Carter," she said quietly as she started boiling the kettle.

"Morning, Julia," I said back to her, a small smile creeping across my face. "How are you?" waiting for her response as I sat at the breakfast bar

"I am perfect, thank you for asking. How about you?" she asked, her eyes on me the whole time.

"Not too bad, is James about?" I asked her, not wanting to pull him from their floor if he had a late night.

"That's good to hear, Carter. He will be down shortly. Is everything okay?" Julia knew I only asked after James when I was in shit, when I needed someone to turn to.

"Yea, just some issues I am dealing with that James is aware of." I smiled weakly at her as I took the steaming cup of coffee from her hands. "Thank you."

I nodded once receiving my cup. I am fully aware Julia probably knows half of what has gone on, but she would never let on, and I would never ask James if he told her. I trust him and Julia with my life.

She plated my usual omelette up and walked quietly out of the room. I took a sip of my coffee and moaned in appreciation as it slipped down my throat like silk. I closed my eyes for a moment, letting the cup warm my hands and soul when I heard James enter the kitchen.

"Morning, boss," he said as he helped himself to a cup and flicked the kettle back on. "Wanna talk about last night yet?" his voice hushed.

I tutted at him and pulled out the stool next to me. He scooped a big spoonful of coffee granules, finishing making his coffee before he took a seat.

"What happened?" he asked before taking a sip of his black coffee.

"I don't fucking know, man," I said frustrated, pushing my hand through my hair.

"She obviously said no to the whole flavours situation," he said with a hint of humour in his voice.

I rolled my eyes as he sat in his seat smirking at me. "Piss off," I snapped at him. He held his hands up at me.

"Okay, so what happened after that?" he asked intrigued.

"She kept going on about being a whore and a prostitute, and that she wasn't that girl. I must admit she was being strong and holding it together, then obviously as you know she crumbled as soon as the car door was shut." I sighed. "Then when we got out, I tried desperately to feel the electricity that I have felt every single time I have touched her, but there was nothing. I feel like I have blown it, that she is repulsed by me and that now that feeling that she must have been feeling is also gone," I said, shaking my head while pushing my uneaten omelette round my plate.

James whistled through his teeth as he spun slightly on his bar stool.

"Man, you are in deep." He sighed, blowing out his cheeks. "But this is what you wanted, isn't it? For her to not want to be one of your flavours so you can move on and focus on Aimee but judging by what you have said and how you are feeling, I take it that isn't the case anymore?" he asked me.

"Nah, I don't want Aimee. I thought I did but I know now deep down that I don't. That part of my life is over. I don't even care if I *never* see another one of my flavours again. Honestly, the way I'm feeling at the moment is how I felt when I caught Rylie cheating. I wanted to take her back so bad, but I couldn't. Male pride and all that, but Freya is different. Freya is mine," I said confidently.

"So, what you gonna do? You gonna come clean?" he asked, helping himself to my now cold and untouched omelette, my eyes burning into him, but he didn't give a shit. He wasn't threatened by me, and I didn't want him to be. He was like my brother.

"I don't know. I need to. I know that much, but I wouldn't even know where to start. Because let's be honest, if I hit her with '*I was only doing this because the woman I thought I was in love with was the woman who cheated on me with your ex, so I wanted revenge*' isn't going to go down to well, is it? Maybe I'll see where things go, see what happens. I am going to see her today, so will see if we can come back from this. If it goes okay, then I will plan on how I will tell her. If it doesn't then no point in me wasting my time in confessing something when the outcome isn't going to change." I took a deep breath. "Does that make sense?" I asked him.

"Yup, completely. I do agree with ya, but either way, mate, I think you should tell her. It'll find its way out. Things like that always do," he said with a mouthful of breakfast. "Damn, my wife is a good cook," he boasted, and I met him with another eye roll.

"What you going to do about your flavours? Someone is due tonight, aren't they?" he asked me.

"Yea, but I'm cancelling them. Not interested in doing this anymore. Yea, the sex is great, I can have it when and where I want and can be as selfish as I want, but after sleeping with Freya, I can't do it anymore. I feel like I already belong to her. She has already claimed me, and the thought of being with anyone else makes me feel physically sick to my stomach." I shook my head before finishing my now cold coffee.

"Well that's one good thing, that you don't want to be that guy anymore. You know what you need to do, mate. But, maybe give her some space, some time," he said quietly before standing up and putting his plate and cup in the sink.

I daren't tell him I tried to call her God knows how many times last night. I was getting myself angry thinking that I have pushed her into the arms of the surfer wannabe. He was a good guy, she deserved a good guy. Not a fucked up arsehole like me.

I was distracted by James. "Anyway, better get on with my work. Don't want to piss the boss off," he jeered at me then gave me a wink.

"James, thank you, mate. I really appreciate it," I said, smiling at him. "Also, can you give me a lift to Freya's this afternoon? Don't really feel like driving."

"Anytime, boss, see you later," he said before walking out of the kitchen and disappearing upstairs.

I put my head in my hands. I needed to think this through. I'm going to head over there, talk it through and see if she is willing to give us a go.

I've got to cancel Luisa tonight, so that's got to be done first.

I nodded at my thoughts and made my way back upstairs to get myself sorted for this afternoon.

-

I got James to drop me outside Freya's apartment and told him I would call him once we were done. I had all intentions of her coming home with me.

I walked up and gave her door a knock. I stood back and waited for her. After a few moments I knocked again, but still no answer.

I pulled my phone out my pocket and called her. No answer.

I could feel myself getting annoyed now. Was she purposely ignoring me?

After calling her for the eighth time, I gave up, but I wasn't going home. I would sit outside her apartment until she got back.

I slid down the wall, next to her front door, with my hands in my hair, going out of my mind. Was she hurt? Had I upset her that much?

I knew she was out with Ethan, James text to tell me he saw her sitting with a blonde shaggy haired looking guy. I bet he just couldn't wait to snatch her from me.

Just as I was about to lose my temper and take it out on the wall, I heard her down the bottom of the stairs. I watched her screw her little nose up at the pizza leaflet that was in her letterbox.

I laughed to myself as I could imagine what was going

through her mind. She started walking up the stairs from the communal hallway and my heart started fluttering as soon as I laid my eyes on her.

She looked great considering how I left her, me on the other hand felt like shit. I wanted to run to meet her at the top of the stairs, scooping her up into my arms and spinning her round before planting a luscious kiss on her perfect, plump lips. But I couldn't. I let my hurt and anger get in the way.

Her eyes focused on me, shocked to see me sitting here. I couldn't see any other emotion through my red haze that was starting to cover my eyes, the rage building.

"Well, look who has returned from her date," I hissed as if the words were poison on my tongue, the bitterness lacing the hurt.

"It wasn't a date." Her voice confident in her answer. "I met my friend for a coffee," she said causally keeping her feet firmly on the ground on the stairs.

"You met *him* from downstairs." I raised my voice, not that I wanted to, but I couldn't control it. I knew I had pissed her off as she was biting back, gripping the bannister tightly.

"Firstly, *him* from downstairs has a name. It's Ethan."

I slowly stood from the floor and made my way over to her.

"I have been sitting here for three hours waiting for you, waiting for you to come home from being with him." I stood so I was now looking over her. My rage slowly fading, losing myself in her stunning, light grey eyes.

I loved how they changed colour. Sometimes they were a sea green, other times they were the grey that I loved.

"I don't want to share you." I breathed, watching her close her eyes as I moved closer to her, our lips millimetres from each other before she whispered, "I don't want to share you, but it doesn't work that way does it?"

I just wanted to kiss her, make her forget last night. I wish I never had that chat with her, I always have to ruin a good thing. I would do anything to go back to last night, to just have a date. I fucked up so bad.

She slowly opened her eyes and looked up at me, her lashes fluttering softly on her skin. Oh I just wanted to make her forget everything. Before I could register what she was doing, she ran her fingers through my hair then slowly down the back of my head, grabbing the tuft at the nape of my neck.

She then pulled my mouth towards her and kissed me. There it was. The electricity. My heart swelled as I felt the current course through me. I wanted to kiss her so much harder, but we kept it slow, soft – but the mood took over me. The shitty night last night was still instilled in my mind, and all I wanted to do was erase it from her memory as well as mine.

I sped the kiss up. I was fierce and hard, my tongue invading hers. My arms wrapped round her as I lost myself in our kiss.

I felt goose bumps all over my body as she slowly stroked down my back. I moved my large hands down to her hips then grabbed her toned, peachy arse. I wanted to lift her up, slam her against the wall and take her right here, right now. I didn't care if anyone saw us. I would gloat if I knew Ethan had watched us, so he knew she was fucking me and me only.

I will do anything in my power to make her see that, to make her see she was made for me. She pulled away, removing my hand from her bum and pulling me towards her flat door.

I wrapped my arms around her waist as she opened the front door. She turned to look at me, her eyes filled with want and need that only I could fill. We didn't have to say anything, my hands were back on her waist lifting her curvy frame up effortlessly and walking through to her bedroom, our mouths covering each other's.

I placed her down and lifted her grey tee over her head then pulled her long, auburn curls out of its messy bird nest of a hairstyle, watching as she shook it loose. My greedy hands were on her tanned body as I drank her in, then pressing my lips against her neck, taking in her sweet scent, then slowly tracing my hungry kisses along her jaw line and over her mouth, then back down to her neck. I was so hard for her. I just wanted to bury myself into her all day.

I heard her let out a deep sigh, "Carter," she murmured. I didn't want to pull my lips off of her.

"Mmm," I responded in a low growl.

"What are we doing? You've made it clear what you want," she said as he pulled away from me, then bit my lip.

"I want you Freya. You want me. Why has this got to be so hard?"

And again I couldn't just tell her the truth, I still had to keep this macho front. She sighed again as she stepped away from me.

"You are the one making it hard. You are being greedy. I'm not enough for you. The fact that you have six girls you alternate between, and then you want to make me a seventh..." she trailed off.

I bowed my head slowly and removed my hands from her body. I couldn't bear to touch her knowing that I couldn't even tell her how I really felt. I was a fucking coward. I didn't even know what to say. what the fuck do you say to the woman you have fallen so fucking hard for when the words have escaped you? I haven't even got the courage to tell her that I don't want anyone else but her.

"Exactly, I'm not enough, you can't even deny it," she said, exhausted by this conversation.

I rolled my sleeve up and checked the time. Shit. I've got to sort this mess out. Luisa is due over soon and I still hadn't cancelled her. I can't do this now. So I done my usual dick move.

"I've got to go. I've got stuff to sort out," I muttered. I couldn't even look her in the eye. I was ashamed of my behaviour, but when you have been a certain way most of your life, you can't just switch back to the way you were before.

Before you had your heart obliterated by a girl.

She stood there, her mouth dropping open, obviously in shock at what I had said. I was in shock with what I had said. I couldn't help myself. I needed to sort my shit out. We could be making love right about now, but she got in my head, and now I am too far into my own head that I can't continue.

My eyes burning into hers, I wanted to grab her and kiss her then throw her on the bed and make her feel what I did. Make her feel exactly how important and special she is to me. How I didn't want anyone else but her.

"You are just going to go without saying anything?" she said, clearly pissed off, shaking her head at my lack of words. "Fine, go," she snapped.

I took a step forward and kissed her on the forehead, taking a deep breath in and remembering her sweet scent before walking out of her bedroom and straight out of her flat. She didn't follow me, she didn't call after me. Yet why would she? I have just blown her out and made some stupid fucking excuse. But, I don't think this is an excuse, I was leaving so I could sort this flavour shit out.

I am done.

Done with being a man whore.

Done of using women to my advantage.

I needed her and only her. And today was the day I was going to finally let go. Let go of my past and move the fuck on with my life.

To move on with Freya.

CHAPTER EIGHTEEN

I paced up and down the pavement while I waited for James. Okay, so it didn't go as I envisaged, but I couldn't make love to her, not until I sorted out this shit I had got myself into.

After a few more minutes I sighed in relief as he pulled up kerbside. I jumped straight in the passenger side and slammed the door.

I could feel James' eyes boring into me, but I needed a moment to chill. A moment to calm myself.

After a few moments, I let out my held breath. "Thanks for getting me," I said quietly.

"No worries, boss man. You were awake. What happened?" he asked, eyes on the road the whole time.

"She was out with Ethan," I snapped, not at James, but at myself for even letting her get to this point where she would want to see him.

"Oh. The surfer wannabe?" he said raising his eyebrows.

"Yup, that prick," I spat.

"Did you talk to her then?"

"Yea, I did. We sort of sorted it, one thing started leading to another, then I stopped. I stopped kissing her, stopped sex from happening." I shook my head at myself.

"I couldn't do it while I still had this arrangement going on with the other girls." I watched as he nodded.

"Think you are doing the right thing mate." James nodded in agreement with himself. "If you want to move forward with her you need to nip all this in the bud."

"I know. I just don't want to be a complete bastard to the other girls, but I know this is what I want," I said quietly as I rubbed my index finger with my thumb. I wanted to turn back and forget all about this, but I needed to get it sorted.

"I just hope this don't come back and bite me in the arse," I said, voicing my concerns.

"What do you mean?" he asked.

"Well, what if the girls get bitter and then start trying to find stuff out about Freya and then try to cause a scene?" I shrugged at him. "Or what if Aimee comes back on the scene? What if she tells Freya what I said as she left the penthouse about not stopping to get back to her and not basically giving a fuck who I hurt in the process?" I started to panic, maybe I should just cut ties now.

"Carter, buddy, calm the fuck down." James chuckled. "You are over thinking this. Keep the girls' sweet, and Aimee, don't stress. She doesn't know that you wanted to use Freya in the first place, does she? You never even knew Freya existed at that moment," he said, watching me as we sat at traffic lights. "You have nothing to worry about. Freya won't know." He smiled at me before continuing to the penthouse.

I just wanted this all to be over now, so I could concentrate on Freya. I needed to get back to her as soon as I could.

It was Sunday evening. I had called all the girls telling them that I would pay them full pay for six months. That way it gives me enough time to work out if what I've got, well hope to have with Freya, is working. If it doesn't, then I can go back to my old lifestyle.

To be honest, the thought of it made me feel sick to my stomach. I hadn't spoken to Freya since walking out. I needed to clear my head and detach myself from the situation.

I felt like an absolute arsehole as I knew I had hurt her. I could see it all over her face, but I had a plan. When she turns up for work tomorrow I will be waiting for her in Jools' office. I am taking her away from You Magazine, so she can work under me. That way I can keep her close, just in case any of my ladies want to get bitter and start shit up, especially Aimee.

James was most likely right, why would Aimee even know about Freya? She wouldn't know about my plan as such, well old plan. I do need to come clean with Freya about it, but not yet. I just want to get to know her a bit more. There is still so much more of her I need to know.

I grabbed myself a beer and turned in for the night. I felt shattered all of a sudden. I flicked the tele on for some background noise to keep me company as I slipped into a deep slumber.

I woke to my alarm; my fingers quickly find the 'off' button on my phone. I stretched and then made my way into my bathroom, starting my day.

I had chosen a charcoal suit with plain white shirt, no need for a tie. Once dressed, I styled my hair and sprayed my cologne. I don't know why but I was nervous. Jools knew I was coming in, and she knew I was taking Freya with me. I don't know how Freya will feel about it, but we will soon find out.

I walked downstairs to my coffee and breakfast and sat alone, scrolling through my work emails and winding myself up at the incompetence of some of my staff. James appeared from upstairs all suited and booted. I felt lucky to have him and Julia in my life. They were like my second family. Talking of family, I really needed to speak to my mum. It had been too long.

"Morning, boss," James said with chirpiness in his voice.

"Morning James, you okay?" I asked as I grabbed my

wallet out of the hallway table.

"Yea all good, you?" he asked as he walked past me, pressing the lift button.

"Yea I'm okay, bit anxious but it'll be fine, right?" I asked with nerves clear in my voice.

"Of course, mate! Cor, I have never seen you like this man." He laughed as we entered the lift together.

"I know! It's foreign to me. I feel uneasy," I admitted as we walked towards the car in the carpark.

"Well, don't. It'll be fine. You and Freya are meant to be. Me and Julia were talking last night. You two are soulmates. Like me and Julia. Honestly, mate, trust me. I can see how much you love her already," he said, flooring me.

"Love?" I stammered out as I sat next to him in the car. "It's not love," I argued back.

"Okay, mate, no fooling us. We know what love is. And you my friend, are in love."

I shook my head at his stupid comment. I had fallen for her, my god had I fallen. But love? I shook away the thoughts and pushed them to the back of my mind. I couldn't be in love. I have never felt what I feel for her with anyone. Not even Rylie.

This woman was a goddess, a perfect angel that I feel like I have broken too much for her to want me back.

But I won't give up without a fight. Like James said, we are meant to be.

I drew in a deep breath as James rolled up outside the offices where You Magazine was situated. I nodded at him as I stepped out onto the pavement. I looked down at my black brogues just to take a moment to slow my breathing before doing my two suit jacket buttons up as I made my way through the glass revolving doors and into the reception.

It was early, but still the place was buzzing. I switched my phone onto silent as I stepped into the lift and made my way up to Jools' small office. I knew Freya wouldn't be here yet as she doesn't start till nine, and she has to get her coffee on the way in the morning.

Man, I couldn't wait to see her. I have missed her so much over the weekend. It feels so much longer than a couple of days. I rubbed my hands together as I started walking towards Jools' office, watching as she stood to greet me.

"Carter," she said smoothly.

"Jools." I accepted her kiss on the cheek before taking a seat opposite her.

"So, you've come to take my best worker then?" she said sipping a black coffee, her eyes on me the whole time.

"That I have. I feel like she has so much more potential, and there is so much more she can give this company. I am sorry to leave you in the shit, Jools, but this is the perfect time to toupee her over to Cole Enterprises," I said, fingers interlinking with each other.

"I understand, Carter, she really is fantastic at her job and picks things up really quickly. I feel like she has been here forever. I am hard on her, but that's just because she shows so much potential. She will go far if she is in the right hands," she said, raising her eyebrows at me.

"That I agree with completely, Jools. I can't wait to see how she fits into my company. I just hope she can cope with a bigger office and work force. It's only you two in this bit as the main part of the magazine is downstairs, which I don't get by the way," I said letting out a light laughter. She joined me before replying, "Neither do I to be honest, but I don't complain. It's not down to me, but you do own us now, so if you want to move us to a more suitable office space it would be much appreciated," she finishes with a smile on her face.

"I promise I'll look into it for you. I do agree that you need a new working space as this isn't sufficient." I smiled back at her.

My heart stopped when I heard the ping of the lift. I stood quickly from my seat, hands in my pocket. I heard the tapping of her heels on the tiled floor. I carried on my quiet chatter with Jools, trying to keep my cool, taking deep breaths as subtly as I could.

I wanted to turn to face her, but I couldn't. My guard would drop, meaning she will see my vulnerability, and I didn't want that just yet. I heard her angelic voice echo off the floor tiles and floor to ceiling glass windows.

"Good Morning, Jools," I heard her call out before I heard the sound of her coffee hitting the floor. I turned to face her. She looked fucking incredible in her tight white shirt and her pencil skirt and them God damn fuckable Louboutin's.

"Oh, I am so sorry, Jools," she said, embarrassed and shocked to see me standing there with her boss. I could only imagine what was going through her head. I watched her amused and bewildered as she bent down as slowly as she could in her tight skirt to pick up the coffee cup.

"I'll go get some tissue," she said quietly, crimson creeping all over her face. I smiled at her as she scuttled off into their kitchen. I heard her running back into the office, my eyes on her again as she bent down again to start cleaning up her mess. I should have really helped her, but to be honest, I loved watching her bent down on her knees. It sent my mind into overdrive about how much I wanted her in front of me, devouring me.

I came back around when she lost her balance and fell onto all fours. Fuck. Her grey, big bambi eyes widened as she focused on me. What the fuck is she doing to me? Was she doing this on purpose?

I couldn't get the dirty thoughts of her out of my head. I went into gentleman mode, bending down in front of her and smirking.

"You really should wear more suitable clothing. That skirt is a bit tight. Maybe I could help you out of it later on

181

after dinner?" I whispered.

Her eyes narrowed as she threw me an evil stare before I took her arm and gently pulled her to her feet. I watched as she brushed herself down and straightened her shirt.

"Sorry again. I will go and make you a fresh coffee," she said. I watched her then move to Jools as she stood from her chair to tell Freya that the coffee wouldn't be necessary and that she no longer had a job at You Magazine, and she is to begin working under me.

Freya didn't know what had hit her. She thought she was losing her job, only then to be told she would be working under me which sent more panic through her.

Jools explained to Freya exactly why this was happening for the next twenty minutes.

"Okay, well, thank you for all you've done for me, Jools. I honestly cannot thank you enough," Freya said before turning to me. "Mr Cole, thank you for this opportunity. I hope I don't let you down."

"I'm sure you won't," I said, but Freya was already out of Jools' office and back at her desk, so I doubt she heard me.

I carried on light conversation with Jools before heading out back to Freya's desk.

"Ready, Freya?" I asked as I stood in front of her, flashing my best smile.

She pushed back from her desk, on her chair, before

grabbing her bag and walking towards the communal hallway where the lift sits. I didn't say anything, just watched her.

She took one last glance over her shoulder, looking straight through me as she smiled at Jools for the last time before walking over to the lift and pushing the button.

I quickly walked up and stood next to her, resting my hand on the small of her back, smiling to myself as I felt the current swarm through me.

I leant closer to her, whispering in her ear, "You look lovely today," before moving back. She didn't say anything. She just stood there trying to show me that she wasn't affected by me, but you could quite clearly see that she was.

I was glad to see James standing kerbside with the doors already opened. I have had a snippet of pissed of Freya, but I think I am about to meet a whole new side of her. I could feel her frustration in her body language and I knew I was going to be getting an earful as soon as we were behind closed doors.

She doesn't realise I have done this to stay close to her, so I can be near her as much as I want to. To make her realise I have changed, to make her fall hard for me.

James greeted Freya, but she stayed silent as she got into to car. I greeted James and shook my head, trying to warn him for what was about to unfold. He nodded and smirked slightly, he was enjoying this a bit too much for my liking.

As predicted, as soon as the door was shut she blew.

"What the hell do you think you are doing!?" she shouted at me. I didn't say anything as I knew there was more coming.

"Who do you think you are, taking me from my job? I loved my job and now, well, I don't even know what I'm going to be doing!!" Again raising her voice.

I inhaled deeply through my nose before saying, "Calm down, Freya, I want you to work for me, so that's exactly what you are doing." My voice coming out with a little more assertiveness than I would have liked.

"I own You Magazine, so If I want to take an employee that I think will benefit my company, I will," I said with a smug grin creeping on my face. She sat back in her chair, her shoulders relaxing as she took a deep breath.

"That's not fair, I was happy in my job, I knew my job. Now, now I don't even know what I will be doing, where I will be working..." she rambled on.

To stop her I placed my hand on her knee. "Baby, please don't stress about that. We are not going to work today, we are going to my place. There's a few things I need to speak to you about before you start Coles Enterprise tomorrow."

She pulled her eyes from me and turned to look out the window.

"Fine," she mumbled.

I took my hand off of her and let her have some stewing

time. She pulled her phone out her bag and started angry typing, no doubt to Laura. I rolled my eyes and pulled my own phone out and started working through my ever-growing list of emails.

After a few moments, I heard her throw her phone into her bag in temper then drop her bag to the floor. I looked up at her to ask if she was okay, but before I could, she held her finger up to her mouth, silencing me. She was making me mad, but mad in a way that I wanted to push her skirt up round her waist and make love to her, making her feel like the queen she is.

My thoughts soon stopped as we pulled up outside the penthouse and I hopped out, taking Freya's hand and leading her to the communal entrance. I loved watching her face as she took everything in, in complete awe.

I greeted the doorman as I walked her through the lavish lobby and over to my private lift. I watched as she fidgeted with her shirt. I knew she was nervous as whenever she was she either fiddled with her clothes or her fingers.

"Don't be nervous," I said calmly. "You have nothing to worry about."

She took my words as an order and dropped her hand before clasping onto her bag handle to clearly give her hands something to do. I could think of a couple of things her hands could be doing to stop her fidgeting. They could be clasped tightly around my cock and pleasuring me into oblivion.

I felt myself go hard just thinking about it and her not having a clue at all as to what was going through my head. I was glad when the lift pinged open. I let her out first as I followed slowly behind her.

She dropped her bag in my hallway and just started wandering towards the windows overlooking the city. I didn't speak, just let her wander and admire my apartment. It gave me a moment to calm myself down from my earlier thoughts.

After she finished her tour, she slipped her shoes off and walked towards me.

"I bought you here to talk, Freya," I said quietly. Now I felt nervous.

She looked deep into my eyes before answering inquisitively, "About what?"

"I want to try... I want to try and just be with you," I said quietly. I could tell she was shocked, but then she started shaking her head at me as if dismissing the idea before we had even given it a shot. Pulling her arm gently so she sat down next to me, I began to speak.

"Freya, please," I begged for her to listen. "After I left your apartment yesterday, I couldn't stop thinking about you. I don't want to lose you. I had a taste of that yesterday when my actions pushed you towards Ethan."

I felt my temper creep up but managed to push my anger back down where it belonged.

"I can't get you out of my head. I've hardly slept, I've

hardly eaten. So, when I left, I called my girls and told them that I needed to work through some things, something I felt very strongly about," I finished, searching her face for some sort of expression but she gave away nothing, just stood there waiting for more, and that's exactly what I did.

I cleared my throat. "So, I said I would put them on six months full pay until I know how this is going. This being me and you." Again I looked at her, waiting for her to say anything.

After a few moments, she put her hand on my knee.

"Carter, I can't let you do that. You have needs, you like to switch it up and not be stuck with the same girl. I get that…"

I moved closer to her, stopping her from finishing her sentence.

"Freya," I breathed in barely a whisper. "I just want you."

CHAPTER NINETEEN

I sat anxiously waiting for her response. She still had hold of my knee, words seemed to escape her. I couldn't take it anymore.

"Say something, please," I pleaded. I needed her to tell me she wanted to try too. That she wanted to make a go of this with me. If she said no, I couldn't cope with the hurt again.

After what felt like a lifetime she finally said, "You've really done that for me".

I took hold of her left hand, squeezing it slightly. "I really have," I said.

She stared at me as if she was taking in every feature I had. It was worrying me as it seemed she was trying to take it all in to remember me.

"Okay," she said quietly. At first, I was unsure of what she was saying okay to, but then it dawned on me, she was okaying for us to give this a go.

"Okay?" I asked, not quite believing it, "Really?" I said

like an excited school boy.

"Let's just take this one step at a time, we've only known each other a couple of weeks. There is still a lot we don't know about each other," she said cautiously.

I nodded in agreement with her. "One step at the time." I smiled at her.

We sat in silence for a few moments, like giddy teenagers before she said, "I would like to know what this new role is that you have for me."

I stood up, suddenly feeling stifled and uncomfortable. I took my suit jacket off and folded it, placing it on the arm of sofa.

"I've got a few new companies Cole Enterprises are looking to buy, and I would like you to be my virtual assistant." I watched her expression change, her eyebrows raised as if she thought I was pulling some joke.

"Hear me out, please," I reassured her. "A virtual assistant is a remote freelancer who helps small companies and consultants with some of the more routine tasks, like writing letters, blogs, columns, press releases and even proof reading. Now, I know you enjoyed the manuscripts, so this would still be in your job description. Most of these companies we buy are in a bad financial state, so there is normally a lot of work to be done, most of that being writing. It's a temporary position, just until they are up and running. You will then have the choice to move into one of our existing companies and enrol in any job."

I took a breath, I couldn't work out if she was interested or not. She looked unsure which made me worry.

"Please, it's just a fill gap," I reassured her. She nodded and agreed that she would work under me with this role and I couldn't wait.

"Now, can we move onto more pressing matters?" I asked, her eyes looking me up and down.

"What would that be then?" she asked all coy, even though she knew exactly what I was getting at.

She stood from the sofa and started to slowly move backwards as I sat myself down, my eyes following her like a lost puppy. Her eyes enlightened with lust.

"Like getting you out of that skirt. I have been wanting to do it since you stepped into Jools' office this morning."

I then stood and slowly made my way over to her, hungry for her and so wanting. She stood with her back pressed on the breakfast bar. She was right where I wanted her.

I clasped her face tightly in my hand before kissing her fiercely. I felt like everything I had felt for the last few weeks was pouring out of me into this one kiss.

Her tongue found mine as she stroked it, a low growl left my throat. She was consuming me, I couldn't get enough of her. I moved my hands from her face and slowly moved them down to her waist before my fingers found the zip on that sexy arse skirt.

I pulled away from her, instantly missing the spark

from our connection. I wanted to see every inch of her, savouring her tanned, luscious curves. I continued to unzip her before tugging at her skirt, letting it fall to her feet. She stepped out of it so elegantly, my eyes trailing up her marvellous legs.

Fuck, I wanted to be in between them making her scream my name. I want it to be only my name that comes from her lips. I will make and claim her as mine. I stepped forward as I started to unbutton her shirt buttons, taking my time, even though I wanted to rip them open and take her right there and then, but I knew I would regret it.

I wanted to take my time and savour every moment with her.

I slid her shirt down her silky, smooth skin and let it fall to the floor, keeping my eyes on her body. I took a step back, so I could take a moment to admire what a fucking rare beauty she was.

My eyes trailed up and down her when I noticed the underwear she was wearing. It was the sexy white lace set she wore on our first date. She looked incredible.

I slowly pushed her auburn locks over her shoulders. I didn't want any of her covered.

She stepped towards me with a look of hunger in her eyes, and it made me horny as hell. There was lust all over her face, her lips parted, her breathing shallow as she planned her next move in her head.

She reached up to my shirt and started un-doing my

buttons, mirroring the same, torturous slowness that I had done with her.

My heart started racing as each button was undone and exposing me, she planted a soft kiss on my chest as she continued to work down to my belt. I knew where this was going. I wanted to stop and just give her pleasure but then again, I didn't.

I wanted to fuck her mouth, I wanted her to be on her knees, devouring me. I smirked as she dropped to her knees in front of me. Fuck, she looked amazing.

Her eyes looking up at mine like an innocent angel as she hungrily pulled my belt from its buckle and pulled my trousers down. She teased me by running her fingers gently along the waistband of my boxers before kissing me delicately. I automatically started playing with her hair, softly twirling her curls around my fingers.

I was so hard, I felt like she would only have to touch the tip with her full lips and I would come all over her pretty fucking face.

This woman.

She sunk her teeth into her bottom lip as she slid my boxers down, her eyes widening as my cock sprung from them. She was so hungry for me, and I was even hungrier for her. There I was, stood stark bollock naked with this goddess on her knees, ready to take all of me into her angelic mouth.

I looked down at her as she took me into her hands and

started pumping me up and down. It felt so fucking good. I felt like I was going to explode. I needed to try and take it slow, I didn't want this to be over already.

As if she could read my mind, she stopped her hand at the base of my cock before taking me into her sweet mouth. I took a deep breath as I tightened my grip around her hair.

"Oh, Freya," I moaned. Her sucks got harder and faster.

How the fuck has she only been with one man? This is the best head I have had, and I've had a few.

I started thrusting my hips faster into her. She pulled me out and flicked her tongue over my tip which pushed me over the edge and closer to my climax. Before I could think about holding off, she took me back into her mouth and continued pumping and sucking me, before she milked me completely, pushing me to my building orgasm.

I moaned out and started thrusting back into her again as I rode my climax out. I shuddered as I came back down to reality, her still on her knees in front of me, her grey eyes burning into mine. She looked so pleased with herself.

"Did you enjoy that?" she said in a silky voice as she pushed herself off the floor.

I didn't wait for her to catch her balance as I pushed her against the breakfast bar. I didn't care if I was too rough, I couldn't hold off anymore.

Yes, that orgasm was fucking amazing, but I needed more.

I covered her mouth with mine. I could taste me on her tongue and it was such a turn on. Not that I needed to be anymore turned on than I already was.

I lifted her effortlessly onto the breakfast bar, spreading her legs apart before running my hand up her back and taking her hair into a tight grip before pulling her head back slightly.

I moved closer to her ear before whispering, "I can't wait to fuck you. I am going to drive you wild."

I heard a small moan leave her lips at my words. I let go of her hair before undoing her bra and letting it fall to the ground then taking her full breasts into my hands before flicking my tongue over her hard nipples and sucking them, which let out another heavenly moan.

I smiled against her sensitive nipples before dropping to my knees. I felt her eyes on me. Her lips parted as her breathing became heavier. I hooked my finger around her lace panties and pulled them to the side exposing her.

I ran my finger down her soaked core before sliding one finger into her.

Fuck, she was so wet.

I started circling my thumb pad over her clit gently. Her moans were intoxicating.

I continued to slide my finger in and out of her at a slow, tantalizing rhythm. I smirked before switching my thumb for my tongue.

She threw her head back as she cried out, "Carter,

stop."

I could feel her tighten around my fingers. I wanted to bring her to orgasm, I slipped my fingers from her as I stood up, grabbing her around the hips and sliding her towards me. Her eyes were full of passion and lust.

I leant over her, pressing the tip of my cock at her opening. I stilled for a moment as I calmed my breathing. I slid into her, hard and fast, her whimpers leaving her lips as I continued to hit her sweet spot, deep inside her.

Her legs wrapped round my waist as I carried on thrusting into her. I could tell she was getting close as she was clamping tightly around me. I had to stop.

I scooped her up and walked her through to the bedroom as I placed her at the foot of the bed. I looked down at her. She was fucking perfect. Just as I was about to push her down on the bed, she took the lead. And it was a turn on.

She pushed me to the bed before straddling me, then taking my hard cock and putting my tip at her opening again as she lowered herself onto me, taking all of me again. A gasp left her mouth as pleasure took over her body and soul.

I felt her eyes burn into my soul as she continued to ride me. I placed my hands on her hips gently as I moved with her rhythm. This wasn't sex now, this was making love.

I sat up and wrapped my arms around her tightly, cradling her as I took her aroused breasts into my mouth as she continued to ride me slowly but deeply.

"Carter." My name slipped off of her tongue in an erotic moan.

"Keep going, please," she begged in a whisper.

I did as she asked.

I rolled my tongue over her sensitive nipples as I hit her with each, deep thrust. It was too much for her and me. I hit into her one final time with a deep, hard thrust as she came undone around me sending me into a soul shattering orgasm.

She was everything to me. Everything I never knew I needed or wanted. She was home to me.

CHAPTER TWENTY

The last few weeks had flown, and I couldn't wait to meet Freya's parents. We were going from strength to strength. I loved her so much but hadn't been brave enough to tell her. I knew she felt strongly for me, but I didn't want to scare her away by telling her my true feelings.

I was spending my first night without her tonight. We had been living at mine and I didn't want to be without her. I had sent her home to pack her bags after she agreed to come to New York with me. I was so excited to be pushing our relationship this step further. I knew she was hesitant about coming, but luckily Laura had coaxed her into the idea.

Lucky for me, Julia packed for me. I did insist but she wouldn't let me.

I felt exhausted all of a sudden. I think it was the apprehensiveness of meeting her parents, I hadn't ever met the parents of someone I have dated. I didn't know how to act, I wanted them to like me, I wanted them to realise I was the right person for Freya. I was also nervous at the thought of spending four to six months in New York with her, but excited at the same time.

I quickly showered and got myself into bed before picking my phone up. My fingers hovered over the screen, debating whether to text her. I wanted to tell her to text me before bed. I didn't want to come across as needy or suffocating but I just wanted to speak to her.

I decided to bite the bullet and quickly text her that I missed her. I smiled as I started to type, my heart beating faster as I continued;

Hey, beautiful, really missing you. I can't wait to see you tomorrow, I just wanted to say I've really enjoyed these last few weeks. Hope the packing is going well, text me before bed. C xx

An hour or so passed and I still hadn't heard from her. I was knackered, but I wanted to stay awake, I needed to hear from her. It had gone eleven when my phone beeped, and of course it was my angel.

Hey, you, just got into bed. I'm missing you, feels weird spending a night without you seeing as we have lived in each other's pockets for the last few weeks. I bet you are fast asleep. I am all packed and bags ready at the door. See you tomorrow, night xx

Her message instantly made me feel more awake. Of course I stayed up. I told her to text me before bed. I wasn't going to fall asleep. I laughed to myself before tapping a message back to her.

Night, baby. I said I wanted you to text me before bed, so I stayed up. See you in the morning. C xx

I instantly relaxed now I had spoken to her. I put my phone on charge and fell into my pillows. My God I felt exhausted.

I woke early as I checked over what Julia had packed for the weekend in Elsworth, and then my trip to New York. I was startled when Julia walked into the bedroom.

"All set, Carter?" she asked as she walked towards me with a folded white tee. "I forgot to pack this, wasn't sure if you wanted it for this weekend?" she asked as she placed it on top of my duffle bag.

"Thank you, Julia." I smiled at her as I unzipped my bag, gently placing it on top.

"How you feeling about meeting Freya's parents? You

excited?" Julia asked softly.

I took a deep sigh. "I am, but I'm anxious. I am taking her back to her past, back to where she got hurt."

Julia looked at me sympathetically. "It'll be fine. Sometimes we all go through things that brings back the hurt we have been through." She took my hand in hers and clasped her spare hand over the top. "It will all be fine, Carter, you will have a lovely time," she soothed as she removed my hand from hers.

"What if Jake is there?" I asked, confiding in her.

"He has moved to London, has he not?" she asked.

"Well, yeah," I stammered. "But, just, what if?" I asked her again.

"Carter, if he is there, he is there. There isn't much you can do about it, but are you going to let that stop you from enjoying your weekend with Freya?" she reasoned.

"No, I suppose not. I have to just keep thinking he won't be there." I smiled as I threw my duffle bag over my shoulder. "Thank you, Julia, as always, for being there when I need you."

"Always, Carter," she said as she stood from the bed. "Have a safe trip and we will see you in a few months," her voice soft as she walked out of my bedroom.

Julia was right. I needed to just enjoy my trip with Freya, then we will be away in New York away from everything. Truth was, I was scared to see Aimee.

I shook the thoughts from my head as I grabbed my

small suitcase and made my way downstairs. James was standing there waiting to take me to Freya's.

"James, I was going to drive myself and Freya to Elsworth but thank you." I shook his hand before walking towards the front door. I just wanted to get Freya now, I missed her.

My heart started thumping as I pulled outside her flat. I left the car and ran up the stairs knocking on her door. Within seconds she swung the door open, her grey eyes glistening, her beautiful smile beaming across her face.

I stepped into the apartment, swooping her up into my arms as I wrapped my arms tightly round her waist, her arms finding their way to my neck as I placed my lips on hers, the electric coursing through my veins. I broke our kiss as I stared intensely at her.

"God, I missed you, Freya," I said into her hair. She smelt divine.

I placed her down gently before grabbing her bags. My eyes went wide when I felt how heavy her suitcase was. What the fuck has she packed?

"Freya what have you packed?!" I said exasperated and clearly strained from her suitcase. God, I worked out, I was strong, but hell, her suitcase was ridiculous.

"These are ridiculous, do you need this much? I said I would buy you new clothes when we get to New York." I scoffed when she rolled her eyes at me. I did say I would buy her new clothes, why couldn't she have listened to me? She was so stubborn.

"Oh hush will you. Just take the bags, Cole," she said with a stupid smirk on her face before letting out a giggle. She made me laugh but I kept it in. I wanted her to think I was annoyed.

"By the way, your bum looks lovely in those chinos," she cooed at me. Little minx.

After a struggle of getting the massive suitcase, two small suitcases and my duffle bag into the boot of my Maserati I sat next to her in the car. She knew I was a stubborn arse, and she was a stubborn arse too, but she was definitely in wind up mood. I put Usher – 82701 on.

"You ready, beautiful?" I said as I placed my hand on her thigh. She nodded back at me, smiling. I couldn't wait for these next few days.

Just me and her.

After a couple of hours in the car with easy chit chat, she directed me to her mum and dad's cottage type home. I pulled into the driveway.

Her mum and dad must have heard to engine cut as they both appeared at the front door before her mum came running down the pathway towards the car. Freya quickly clambered out as I followed behind her.

I heard her mum shouting, "Harry, Harry! Our baby's home, she's home!"

I felt my insides melt as Rose embraced her daughter,

squeezing her tightly as her father stood on and watched. Her mum was beautiful for an older lady. I could see where Freya got her looks from. The same auburn hair her daughter has was swept off her face, her deep blue eyes soft and full of love for her little girl.

Her dad was about five foot nine, six foot max, he was stocky, broad shoulders and built like a brick shit house. Given his age, I am sure he can still throw a punch or two. His tanned skin radiated as it was his turn to embrace his daughter.

"Baby face," I heard him mumble as he held her tightly.

I instantly felt a pang of sadness. I missed my dad. Yea, he was an arsehole, but he was still my dad. I missed having a father figure in my life. He wasn't loving like Freya's dad, he was cold. Everything was like a business transaction to him, almost like he wasn't capable of love. As much as I thought he was an arsehole, I still loved him, and I guess I always craved a little more love from him in return. But I never got that from him.

I was distracted when her dad walked across to me. "You must be Carter," he said to me, his voice laced with authority. He actually intimidated me. No one had ever done that apart from my dad.

"That's correct, sir. It's a pleasure to meet you, Mr Greene." I held my hand out, waiting for her dad to take it. It felt like a lifetime before he did, and I studied him the whole time.

His mannerisms and tone were old school. I knew his kind. No sleeping in his daughter's bedroom, no sex before marriage, asking of father's permission.

I let out the breath I had been holding when he took my hand firmly and met my handshake. As we broke our contact he nodded at me before making his way to help me with the suitcases.

I smirked as I caught him having a look at my car. I looked over my shoulder to see that Freya was watching me as her mum walked over to me and embraced me in a motherly hug. My heart warmed again. I felt like it was glowing with the love I was feeling in this situation. I felt like this was my home. Even though it wasn't I have always longed for this family unit which I have never had.

My family life was all about tiptoeing around my dad, always afraid of the mood he was in. Never knowing how he had treated my mum that day, never knowing what the day would bring.

I watched Rose walk into the house as I walked down the pathway with Harry.

"If you want, you can take her for a spin," I said quietly to him, nodding at my car. I watched his face light up at my offer.

"I would like that, but only of course if you don't mind," he said back to me dropping Freya's mammoth suitcase by the front door. "What the bloody hell has she packed in here!?" he asked me. I shrugged my shoulders at him.

"Not a clue, I asked the same thing. It's soooo heavy." I laughed, and he joined me in a light chuckle.

"She is a nightmare," he said before picking it back up again and putting it inside the door by the stairs. He wandered through to the kitchen to meet his wife and daughter. I took this moment to stand and just take everything in.

The low wood beams made the cottage, the cream walls throughout made it feel homely and warm. The old fire sitting in the lounge area with their tanned chesterfields sitting neatly around a cream rug with a matching arm chair pointing directly at the tele.

It wasn't much but I could easily give everything up and wake up here every morning with Freya.

I walked through to the kitchen and there was a black range stove sitting to the right of the oak archway that lead you from the dining room to the living room. The units were shaker kitchen units, slightly off white. I wasn't sure whether it was intentional or just years of wearing. The worktops were black granite, they looked new, but I knew Freya said her mum was OCD with cleaning, so it could be that she took care of them.

The floor was wooden and continued from the living room. There was a farmhouse style round table and chairs where Freya and her father were now sitting. I took a seat next to Freya at the immaculately laid table. Real china plates and tea cups were laid out for us. In the middle were fresh finger sandwiches and a massive pile of biscuits. I was starving, and I couldn't wait to get tucked in.

Once lunch was finished, Rose showed us upstairs. I had to duck as I walked down the narrow cottage hallway as the ceilings were so low.

Freya's bedroom was to the left as you came up the stairs, Rose and Harry's opposite hers, then the main bathroom to the left of the main bedroom then at the end all on its own was the spare room.

I listened as Rose told me that Harry wouldn't want us sharing a room and that she had made the spare room up down the end of the hall. I assured her that I respected Harry's rules and wishes and I was happy to sleep in the spare room while I was here.

I gave Freya a peck on the cheek as I walked towards my room, so I could unpack. Once I got to my room I looked over my shoulder and saw her disappear into her room with her mum. I smiled to myself as I started to unpack my neatly, organised case that Julia had sorted for me. It didn't take me more than ten minutes to unpack and put my clothes away in the wardrobe.

I walked down the hallway to see Freya's door shut. I could hear her mum and her talking so didn't want to interrupt. I made my way downstairs to see Harry sitting in the lounge flicking through the tele. I nodded as I sat down on the chesterfield next to him.

"Hey," he said taking his eyes off of the screen to acknowledge me.

"Hi," I said. "Freya and Rose are unpacking her suitcase, don't mind if I join you, do you?" I asked hesitantly.

"Of course not, but why don't we go down to the local pub. They could be up there for *hours,*" he exaggerated and dragged out the *hours.*

"Sounds good, let me get my shoes on," I said as I pushed myself off the sofa, Harry standing after me and switching the tele off. After a few minutes, we walked quietly through the village.

"This is such a beautiful place, Harry. I would never want to move if I lived here," I muttered

"I know. Me and Rose have lived here most of our lives. I love that everyone knows each other. Freya was always looked out for, we never had any worry with her." His smile small as he reminisced.

"Then that prick had to ruin it all and had to drive her away." His tone changed, his voice was clipped.

"I would never forgive him. I always vowed that if I saw him I would beat him to a pulp, but every time I did see him Rose stopped me and told me to think of Freya. I couldn't cause any more heartbreak for her." He stopped in his tracks and faced me. "Don't hurt her, Carter. I can't see my baby go through anymore heartbreak. The thought of someone else hurting her after what Jake did to her, I just couldn't imagine what it would do to her," he said as he placed his arm on the top of mine and gave it a squeeze.

"Come on, let's go have our beer," he said, removing his hand then gently patting me on the back as we walked into the village pub.

I wanted to tell him about what my intentions were with his daughter, but I couldn't. How could I tell him I wanted to obliterate his princesses' heart for my own benefit? I couldn't. I had agreed not to go ahead with the plan, I agreed to be with only Freya. But this just made me realise even more that I needed to tell Freya the truth. I won't do it this weekend, not with Laura's wedding and the fact that Harry would fucking kill me. I would wait till New York. When we were far from home.

CHAPTER
TWENTY-ONE

We were only in the pub for an hour, but it was nice to have some one-on-one time with Harry. I touched softly on my father and my mother, and my relationship with them both. He was interested in my business which was nice. I explained that it wasn't my dream to take over from my father, but after being forced into it, and then him passing away, I felt I couldn't walk away.

We spoke sport, he told me he supported Tottenham Hotspur and asked if I liked anyone. I told him I wasn't into football, more of a rugby man myself. We touched on hobbies and I said apart from working and spending time with Freya, I didn't really have any.

I liked the odd game of golf every now and again, Harry also told me he enjoyed a game of golf and would love to have a game with me. I had only known him a couple of hours, but I instantly felt a connection. Like he was the father figure I have always needed and wanted. Being a ruthless business man at the young age of twenty-three was not what I had in mind and I hadn't always known what to do or whether I was making the right choices in the last ten years, but it was nice to know that if I could, I could speak to Harry.

He didn't seem like the type of guy that would turn me away. Unless I hurt his daughter obviously.

We walked back to the cottage in quiet chatter. I took in the picturesque surroundings around me. I just couldn't get enough of the cobbled streets, the little bridge and flowing stream that ran through the entire village.

It had just gone midday as we got to the cottage and I couldn't wait to see Freya. As Harry opened the door I saw her sitting on the sofa, she was such a picture. I could never get over how beautiful she was, she was out of this world.

I constantly felt like I needed to pinch myself, worried I was going to wake from this perfect dream that I felt like I was living in.

Harry distracted me from his daughter as he said, "Go take a seat, son, I will grab us a beer from the garage," then slapped me on the back before walking through to the garden.

Son.

Such a bittersweet moment. I had instantly bonded with Freya's dad, and I felt like I finally had a dad back in my life.

My icy heart was thawing by the minute, I felt so overwhelmed. I made my way over to the sofa, kissing my girl on the cheek as I sat down next to her.

"Hey all okay?" I asked. I felt giddy. Not sure if it was the couple of beers, the fact Harry called me son or being completely besotted with Freya.

She smiled at me. "All fine here thanks, what about you?" she asked.

I nodded. "Yup, all good. I love it here, why did you ever want to move away?" I watched as she rolled her eyes at me.

"You know why, Mr Cole," she said, with a hint of sarcasm in her tone. Of course I knew, I just don't understand why she would want to throw this all away.

"How many have you had?" she asked, her eyebrows raised as she was trying to read my expression.

"Only a couple," I said giving her a wink. I saw the silly smirk on her face, I knew she found me funny. Our moment was shortened by Harry walking back in with a pack of four beers. He sat in the armchair then placed the tins on the table.

"I bought these just for you, Carter. You know, what with you being Aussie and all that."

"Dad." Freya reacted shocked at her dad's comment. I looked at the fosters on the table taking me back many years ago when I had first met Louis and he made the comment that we liked fosters just because we were Aussies. Truth was, I still hated the taste, but I couldn't tell her dad that. I would just drink them and be grateful.

"What?" Harry reacted to his daughter. "He is an Aussie, aren't you, Carter?"

All I could do was laugh at him. "That I am!" I said as I took a tin off of him

"Cheers!" we said as we clunked our tins together before Harry switched the cricket on and we fell into easy conversation about that.

I don't know how long I had been watching cricket with Harry for, but I looked to the side of me and noticed Freya had gone. I excused myself and made my way upstairs, her door was pulled to, so I knocked gently before pushing it open slowly.

"Hey, only me," I said quietly as I walked into her room.

"Hey," she replied, her beautiful smile creeping onto her face. "I just had an email from Jools, my old editor letting me know that she is stepping down." I took a seat next to her on the bed.

"Yeah, I heard about that. Her husband isn't very well so she's focussing on him at the moment and not the magazine. I told her that her job will be there for her, if she decides to come back."

I see her check her emails on her laptop, her eyebrows pulling together as she frowned at her screen.

"That's nice of you," she muttered as she closed the lid of her laptop down. I watched as she flopped down onto her bed, her pillow snuggling round her head.

"It feels weird being in my old room," she said while staring at the ceiling. I laid down beside her.

"I bet. I wish I still had my first room in Australia," I mumbled. I felt her turn her head to look at me.

"I bet you have some good memories from there," she said before reaching for my hand, knowing how much I hated my childhood. I turned to face her and smiled I then leant forward and placed a soft kiss on the tip of her nose.

"Oh what I would do to you if we were alone," I whispered to her. It's true, I would take my sweet time savouring every moment with her.

She didn't say anything, she didn't have too, I could see how my words had affected her. Instead, she lifted my arm up and snuggled into my chest. I then bought my arm down and wrapped it around her, pulling her closer to me not wanting her to break the contact. We laid in silence, neither of us needing to say anything.

I felt a pressure on my stomach and chest and I couldn't work out where it was coming from. I was in a deep sleep and couldn't work out if I was dreaming the pressure or it was actually happening. Then I felt soft butterfly kisses along my jaw line which bought me from my sleep, my eyes flickering open when I saw her beautiful grey eyes looking deeply into mine.

"Hey, handsome." She smiled. "Nice sleep?" she asked me as I reached my arms above my head and stretched myself out.

"It was a mighty fine sleep," I mumbled still in a sleepy state. She pushed herself up gently and sat straddled over me, her eyes staying on mine.

"So, Mum and Dad have gone for an Italian in the village and would like us to meet them down there," she said softly. I smiled at her.

"That sounds fab, I'm starving," I admitted. I went to move but she pinned my arms back into the bed and shook her head gently.

"We've got the house to ourselves," she said silkily. Oh, I knew where this was going the little minx. She leant down and kissed me slowly teasing me with her tongue. Her kisses bought me back to reality. I wanted to take control of her. I tried to release my arms but that only made her push down harder. I pulled from our kiss.

"What about what your Dad said? I respect what he asked, baby," I crooned. I couldn't stop myself getting hard just looking at her.

"I know you do," she purred at me. "But we wouldn't be long, plus they aren't here..." she trailed off then let go of my hands, then placing them on my stomach as she slowly pushed my tee up his body.

I put my hands onto her hips then slowly moved them down to her thighs as I pushed her little dress up around her waist. I inhaled a sharp breath; her body was incredible. She startled me as she pushed onto her knees as she greedily undone my belt and trousers as she slid them down my legs, then making her way to my boxers and springing me free.

Her eyes hungrily devouring me. I pushed her panties to the side, pulling her down onto me. There was no need for foreplay, she was soaked. I entered her softly and slowly savouring every minute. I could never get enough of her, the feeling of her taking every inch of me was heaven.

I slowly thrust into her, her hips moving with me as we built each other up to our impending orgasm. Sex with her was like nothing I had ever had before. She completely intoxicated me, consuming my every want and need.

I took her breast into my hand and started softly kneading them before rolling her hard nipple in-between my finger and thumb as I started to pick up the pace. My thrusts were faster and harder as I hit up into her, hitting her sweet spot that made her moan.

I wrapped both arms around her, keeping her close to me as I continued thrusting into her, her head resting on mine as we got closer to our high together.

She covered my mouth with hers as our kiss matched our tempo. It took one last thrust into her as I bought her to her climax, and she bought me to mine, moaning into my mouth as she came hard around me.

We walked hand in hand not saying much between us as she led us to Bella's the Italian. Her mum and dad were sitting there, looking rosy cheeked. Obviously, the wine had hit them.

"Hey," Freya said as we sat down as Harry ordered us a bottle of wine. I was so content, I couldn't imagine anything ruining this weekend.

CHAPTER TWENTY-TWO

It was the evening before Laura's wedding. Freya was going for a bridal party sleepover which meant I was staying back at Roses and Harry's. Freya had said I could stay in a bed and breakfast If I preferred but I didn't want to, I liked spending time with her parents.

The last few days had flown by, and as much as I was looking forward to Laura and Tyler's wedding, I couldn't wait to whisk her away to New York. I didn't want to share her anymore.

I made myself and Freya a cup of tea and left it on the side to cool. I made my way upstairs to check on my angel to see if she needed any help. I leant on the door frame, just drinking her in as she eyed me up and down, smiling at me which made her eyes light up.

I walked over to her and kissed her on the cheek.

"I'm going to miss you tonight, it's weird not staying with you in my own house, but to sleep here with your Mum and Dad while you are Laura's feels really weird." I laughed.

"I know, it is weird, I totally understand if you want to go to a bed and breakfast." There it was again, that offering of a B&B. A little smile crept onto my face.

"No, baby, I want to stay here. It's only one night. Next time I see you, you'll be walking down the aisle."

I saw the pure shock on her face as her eyes flicked back and forth to mine. I couldn't work out what she was thinking. Shit, had I scared her? My mind started racing as I tried to think of something to deter the conversation, but I couldn't think of anything, except I said, "I can't wait," moving closer to her, leaning down and kissing her on her lips.

I would never tire of kissing her.

"Do you need help packing anything?" I asked her, trying to take her mind off of what I just said. She shook her head at me.

"I'm basically done I think," she said as she looked around the room. "Laura has my dress and accessories. I have packed my pyjamas, toiletries and bits like that so, yeah, I think I am done." She smiled back at me.

I moved past her to grab her small suitcase and walked it downstairs for her and left it by the front door.

"Thank you," she muttered behind me. "So, what are you doing tonight?" she asked me. "Me and your Dad are going to the pub, then I think your Mum is meeting us down there

once she is back from book club, so we can all have

dinner." I smiled.

"That sounds nice, I'm jealous," she said quietly.

"Come on, I'll walk you to Laura's." Smiling at her as I picked her suitcase up, she laughed at my offering.

"Honestly, it's okay, you'll get lost," she said.

Sighing I replied, "I won't get lost, worst comes to worst, I will put your Mum and Dad's address in my phone."

She nodded reluctantly at my comment. I waited as she said bye to her parents. I opened the front door for her as she approached me.

"After you," I said quietly, waiting for her to walk past me as I closed the door behind us. I scooped her little hand into mine.

"I'm really looking forward to New York, thank you for giving me the opportunity." she said squeezing my hand gently. I softly rubbed my thumb across the back of her knuckles.

"I'm glad you are coming too, I can't wait."

It was the truth, I couldn't wait.

Everyday waking up with her and falling asleep next to her. This was all I ever wanted before I was broken to the point I didn't think I could be fixed.

After a short walk we were outside Laura's parents' house. It was a beautiful town house, a bit like my own but instead of being tucked away on the busy streets of London, we were in the idyllic town of Elsworth. They had a huge lawn out the front with a beautiful cherry blossom tree which had an old swing tied to the branches.

I smiled. This seemed like the perfect place to bring children up. Still, I would have taken the cottage over this. There's something about that cottage that I loved.

I watched as Freya rang the doorbell, her still gripping my hand tightly while squeezing it again. I couldn't work out if she was nervous or just trying to re-assure me. I jumped in my skin as Laura swung the front door opened and let out a high pitched squeal, making me wince. I felt like she had penetrated my ear drum. I put my index finger in my ear and gave it an itch.

"Anyone would think she was excited," I said in a teasing manner. I watched as she came bounding towards us like a hyped puppy then throwing her arms around both of us as she sung 'I'm getting married in the morning' at the top of her lungs.

Once she finally let us go, watching her jump up and down like a kid who had too many E numbers, she welcomed myself and Freya into her home. I took a quick glance around the grand hallway as I watched Laura's parents appear, taking Freya into a warm embrace.

After a few short words exchanged, they turned to introduce their selves.

"You must be Carter. I am Lucinda, this is Gary." She smiled at me before kissing me on the cheek then stepping aside so her husband could shake my hand.

"So you are in the buying business?" Gary asked inquisitively. I watched as Lucinda stepped back towards Freya taking that as her cue to leave.

"Yes, I am, why do you ask?" I answered his question a bit hesitant. I felt uneasy talking business with someone I hardly knew on a personal level.

"Follow me," he said softly as he wrapped his arm around my shoulders and walked me into their lounge area, pouring us both a whisky before handing it to me.

I didn't decline, but I didn't really want to be drinking seeing as I was due to go out with Freya's dad soon.

"Now, my problem is that I have a small company that I took over a little while ago in the shipping market, but unfortunately I can't seem to get it up and running off the ground. Everything I am doing seems to be failing, and I feel like I am running it into the ground again," he admitted as he let out a deep sigh before taking a sip of his drink. I didn't say anything, just mirrored his actions.

"I don't know where I am going wrong. I'm not sure if it's something you can help me with at all or whether I am better to just auction it off the highest bidder." He shrugged. "I don't really want to let the company go as that could mean the workers lose their job too." He shook his head at his impossible task.

I took another sip of the dark liquor before I answered him. "To be honest, I don't know how much I will be able to help, but I am happy to get my finance team to give you a call to see if we can find the loop hole that seems to be getting through somehow. Then, if they find anything, we can move forward and see if we can get it back up and running. Shipping is such a big industry, it would be a shame to see another business go bust. I am off to New York for a few months for work, but I will pass all your details over to my secretary and I will get her to give you a call to schedule a meeting with my financial team and we can go from there. How does that sound?" I asked.

"That's brilliant, thank you, Carter. Now, we better go back through. God knows what the girls were getting up to." He smiled as he patted me on the back.

I chucked the rest of the whiskey back before placing it back on his drink stand and making my way to the grand hallway. Lucinda was standing at the bottom of the stairs, looking up and listening to the racket that was Laura.

"I am scared she is going to get paralytic the night before her wedding," she admitted.

"Don't be silly, Luc," Gary said as he stood behind her, squeezing her shoulder in a comforting reassurance.

"I'm sure Freya will keep her in check. I've never seen her drunk," I admitted, frowning at the ground.

"Oh, I'm certain you will see her drunk tomorrow. She is a wild one." Lucinda giggled as she stepped towards me. "It was lovely meeting you. You seem to make Freya very happy." She beamed at me.

"Thank you, I do try," I said in response.

"She deserves the world that girl, after what that cheating rat done to her." She sighed. "Anyway, enough about the past. Thank you for making her so happy."

All I could do was smile at her kind words, even though it was true I didn't feel I deserved them after what I had originally planned to do to get revenge on her. But that was all in the past now, a distant memory.

"Well, thank you so much for having me, it was lovely meeting both of you," I said loudly, hoping Freya heard.

We hadn't said goodbye and I didn't want to leave without talking to her.

Just as I was about to accept she hadn't heard, she came running down the stairs and threw herself at me from the bottom step. I caught her, wrapping my arms tightly around her waist, her legs locking around me as she leant in to kiss me.

"See you tomorrow," I said quietly, our faces close, my warm breath on her face. Her breath was laced with the slight smell of champagne.

"I'll miss you," she replied, her voice laced with slight sadness that she was spending the night without me.

I wanted to take her mind off of it, I didn't want her feeling sad. I leant in for one more kiss. I lingered slightly not wanting to break our connection, but I knew I had to. She pulled away and I let out a quiet whimper at the loss of her. I didn't want her knowing, so I shrugged it off.

"Now, go have fun. Text me before you go to sleep and

no getting drunk," I said sternly as I placed her down.

She stood looking giddy and drunk me in as she held onto the stair bannister as I stood with my hand on the front door handle.

"Gary, Lucinda, it was a pleasure meeting you. Gary, next time you are in town let me know and we will have that game of golf," I said smiling as Gary nodded at me. "I'm sure I can help you," I finished off by saying. Gary thanked me again and shook my hand while Lucinda came over and gave me a kiss goodbye on the cheek.

"Enjoy your evening ladies," I shouted up at Laura who was hanging over the stairs bannister.

"Bye, Carter!" she shouted down, I laughed at the thought of what she was going to be like in a couple of hours once the champagne had kicked in. Then my eyes found my queen, the one who held my heart.

My eyes warming as I kept them on her. "See you later, baby," I said smoothly, winking at her before leaving the house closing the door quietly behind me.

I took in a breath of the crisp early evening air as I made my way back to Harry and Rose's. I was proud of myself that I didn't need to use my phone once to find my way back.

I was greeted by Harry as I knocked on the cottage door.

"You ready to go, son?" he asked me, stepping out of the cottage.

"Yup, I'm all good to go," I said as he closed the door behind him, both of us walking down the cobbled pathway towards the local pub. I was looking forward to our evening together, I could actually get used to a life like this. We were in the pub within five minutes as we took our seat at Harry's normal table.

"Pint, Carter?" he asked.

"Please," I responded. "Let me get it, please, you got the last lot when we were here," I pleaded with him.

"Not a chance." He shook his head as he walked towards the bar, ordering two pints and a couple of packets of crisp. He returned within minutes, placing the cool beer on the beer mat in front of me.

"Thank you again, Harry," I said as I held my pint glass up before putting it to my lips and taking a big mouthful.

"Did you meet Gary and Lucinda?" Harry asked me as he took a sip of his beer before opening a packet of the crisp and offering me one. I politely accepted his offer and ate it before responding.

"Yeah, I did. They seemed really nice. Gary asked if I would be able to help him with a failing business he took over, so I said I would look into it for him and if I could help I would," I said proudly.

"That's kind of you, but just be careful. His business trades can be a bit dodgy, so just make sure you look into the history of it before you put too much time and effort into a dead end," he said reassuring me.

"No problem, I will get my finance team on it once I'm in New York," I said, nodding at him.

"Ah, yes, New York. You're taking my baby face away from me for a few months, how you feeling about it?" he asked boldly, his eyes on mine.

"I'm looking forward to it. I know it's soon and we haven't known each other for that long but I am glad she accepted my offer. Your daughter is really good at her job and I want to see her succeed. I know she will shine at this task, then when she is home I have told her she is free to choose any other job within my company, if she wants to change," I said. "I think she was so brave upping and leaving everything she knew. Her family, her job, her friends and her old life. I always wonder what I would do if I ever was faced with an impossible situation," I said trying to gauge Harry's expression.

"Brave and stupid," he said bluntly. "She shouldn't have run away because of him. She was working her way up the ladder, she was starting to make a name for herself in the law department, but he went and ruined it and drove her away." He sighed.

"Don't get me wrong, I am grateful that she met you and you have given her a wonderful opportunity, but I was scared she was going to lose herself, but I can see that she is excelling in her work and I feel that's down to you, Carter, so thank you," he said as held onto his beer glass tightly.

"I just hate him so much and everything he done to

her. She was so different when she was with him. High school sweethearts and he seemed to overpower her. She had no confidence when she was with him. He brought out the worse in her and it was awful to see as a father. You can imagine how Rose felt. He took her away from us. We rarely saw her, and their cottage was literally down the road." He sighed.

"I'm sorry bringing this up, but I can vent to you because I can see how much you love my daughter." He looked at me willing for me to agree with him.

"I do, Harry. I loved her from the moment I saw her for the first time. Don't get me wrong, I have been a bastard in my lifetime, a lot of it due to my upbringing and then I had my heartbroken when I was in university and I vowed never to love again, then I met Freya. I can honestly say she is the love of my life, and one day, I will ask her to be my wife. Obviously with your blessing. I would never ask without your blessing. But I do promise, I will make her happy and look after her like the way she deserves. She is one of a kind and I will never let her go. I promise you I will be the best man I can be," I said letting out a deep breath.

"I know you will, Carter. I can already see the difference you have made in the last few weeks, so thank you. Thank you for making my baby girl happy again and bringing her back from the shell of herself. Honestly, we are so grateful. So again, thank you." We held our pint glasses up and clinked them together.

And it was true. I vowed to make his princess the happiest she had ever been.

CHAPTER TWENTY-THREE

After we sunk a couple of pints we saw Rose walk in. Harry stood from his seat and kissed her on the cheek welcoming her into open arms.

"Carter, darling," she said as she kissed me on the cheek and took her seat next to us. Before Harry could get up, I quickly moved over to the bar, ordering another two beers and glass of white for Rose. As I walked over with the drinks I saw Harry glare at me.

"Sorry, Harry, I saw my opportunity and I went for it. Plus, you are letting me stay under your roof and you haven't let me put my hand in my pocket once." I smiled at him as I took my seat.

"Thank you, Carter," he said before handing me a menu. Dinner passed quickly as we sat and spoke about Freya mainly and just how wonderful she is. Harry summoned the waiter over for the cheque and within moments it was placed in the middle of the table. I saw Harry's eyes dart to mine, mine darting to his before we both put our hand on the bill. I knew he was a proud man, but it was the least I could do.

"Harry, may I? Please?" I asked. I don't think I had ever been so polite. I was normally an arsehole, but I couldn't be that way with them.

"Fine," he groaned as he sat back in his chair and took a sip of his beer as I placed my card down and waited patiently for the waiter to return. I left my chair first, pulling Rose's out for her as she stood and took Harry's hand as she thanked me then kissed her husband.

They had such a wonderful relationship that I could only wish for. Freya had all the good qualities of her parents, so I was certain we would love just as fiercely as they did.

I walked through the pub part of the restaurant when I saw Harry freeze and Rose gasped. It wasn't until I nearly bumped into them that I realised who they were staring at. It was Jake and Aimee.

My heart was thumping through my chest. I could hear the blood flow rushing through my ears as my heart went into overdrive with sheer panic and anxiety.

Aimee's eyes widened as she took me in, then looked up and Jake whose hands were balled into fists. I placed my hand on Harry's shoulder as I instantly felt like I needed to protect him, to let him know I was here and that I had his back no matter what.

Jake eyed Harry, keeping his stare on him. What did Freya, and Aimee for that matter, see in this prick? He was an absolute weed.

He looked like the slime ball type. Dark hair pushed back with way too much gel in. His teeth crooked beyond help of a brace, his skin pale and pasty, his eyes dull. But maybe that was the realisation of what he lost when he decided to do the dirty on Freya, when he decided to rip her innocent heart from her chest and stamp all over it.

It felt like we had been staring for ages, no one saying a word when I saw Aimee lean up and whisper in his ear. An evil grin appeared on his face as his eyebrows knitted together. He walked past us, scoffing at us as he did. What a bellend. I ushered Rose out of the pub as Harry stormed out.

"Harry, calm down," she said as she caught up with him.

"I can't, Rose, he makes me so angry," he snapped. Rose's eyes fell to the floor. I felt awkward but didn't want to leave them.

"I'm sorry, darling. You know what he does to me," he said grovelling.

"I know, but don't take it out on me. Look how happy Freya is now. She looks like a different woman and that's all thanks to what happened, and Carter." Rose rubbed her husband's shoulders before turning to me.

"Honestly, Carter, you brought our daughter back to life and we are forever in your debt. Because she deserves to be happy, as do you," she said smiling at me. I felt a pang of guilt shoot through me. Guilt because I still hadn't told Freya my intentions. I was so scared. Scared because I knew she wouldn't take it lightly, it could end us. And I wasn't ready for that to happen.

I wasn't lying when I said I would make her my wife, because I will. Nothing will stop me or take her away from me.

"Thank you, Rose," I said, grateful for her words. Just when I thought she had finished, she opened her mouth to talk again.

"And as for that trollop." I was interrupted in my thoughts. "Well, they deserve each other with her cheap looking bags and shoes." She shook her head. I nearly choked on the air I was breathing in. If only she knew how expensive the bag and shoes were.

"You okay, Carter?" she asked concerned as I was still coughing trying to catch my breath.

"Yeah, sorry, I am fine." I held my hand up and smiled as I followed them down the cobbled streets. I just wanted to get back to theirs now and speak to Freya.

I was glad when we walked through the cottage front door. I wished Harry and Rose goodnight as I made my way upstairs to my room. I looked at the time, it was gone eleven. I couldn't believe how late it was and how tired I felt. My phone buzzed, when I looked it was my angel.

Hey, baby, I hope you had a nice night with my parents and they didn't grill you too much. I miss you so much, can't wait to see you tomorrow. Dream of me, I'll dream of you xx

I pressed the call button on her text message, I wanted to hear her voice.

"Hello," she answered sheepishly.

"Hey, you okay?" I asked her, concerned at how she answered the phone.

"I am now I have heard from you," she said. I could hear her beautiful smile in her voice. "How was dinner? Are my parents okay? I was meant to call them, but it's been so hectic."

It was my turn to smile down the phone.

"It's fine, they understand. Dinner was lovely, it's a really nice pub." I heard her let out her breath. "Guess what though?" I said.

"What?" she asked, I could hear the nerves in her voice. Balls, should I not say anything? I can't not, can I? I need to tell her.

"We bumped into Jake as we left the restaurant." I stopped as I heard her breath catch, her breathing fastened at what I had just said.

"Babe, you've gone quiet on me," I said trying to get her to talk.

233

"Sorry, just wasn't expecting that," she said quietly as I sighed. I shouldn't have told her.

"Well, it bothered him seeing me with your parents. I just wished you were on my arm. His face was a picture, imagine what it would have been like if you were with me." I laughed nervously hoping she would laugh too.

"Anyway, beautiful, get some sleep. I can't wait to see you tomorrow," I said like an excited school kid.

"I can't wait to see you either. I will see you in the church, Mr Cole," she said seductively. I am sure she was trying to mask how she was really feeling.

"Night, baby, sweet dreams," I said as I laid into bed.

"You too," she said as she shut the phone down.

Fuck, I muttered. I shouldn't have fucking said anything. Now I know she was going to be worrying all night, and it was all my fault.

I woke after a shitty night's sleep. I couldn't stop thinking about the worry I had put Freya through. I felt like I was between a rock and a hard place. I didn't want to lie to her, but part of me didn't want to tell her about running into Jake because of this reason. I pulled myself out of the single bed and walked cautiously downstairs. I felt anxious. I knew it was because she wasn't here.

"Morning, dear," I heard Rose's soft, warm tone.

"Morning, Rose." I smiled at her as I walked towards the kitchen. "Morning, Harry." I nodded at Freya's dad.

"Morning, son." He smiled back at me. *Son.* That bittersweet nickname that bought back so much heartbreak but so much love at the same time.

"Tea?" I was awoken from my heartache.

"Please," I said, my eyes glowing at her. Freya was so lucky to have these wonderful parents.

Within minutes I had a steaming hot cup of tea in front of me and two slices of toast with thick butter and jam. I couldn't remember the last time I had jam on toast, I always had the omelette.

We sat in light chitter chatter before I headed upstairs to get showered and dressed. I asked if Freya's parents wanted to jump in before me, but they kindly declined and told me to go first. I didn't want to take the piss, so I literally had the quickest shower I have ever had. I towelled myself down then wrapped the towel round my waist before walking into my bedroom.

I opened the small, single wardrobe in the small box room I was staying in and pulled out my suit bag, slowly unzipping it before getting myself dressed. I tucked my shirt in that Rose had offered to iron last night for me, even though I politely denied twice, but after the third time I didn't want to cross her.

I chuckled to myself at her face when I told her no. She reminded me of Freya. Her eyebrows pulled in, but her gaze intense as if she was burning into my soul.

An hour later we were all ready to leave for the wedding. God, I couldn't wait to see her. We sat quietly on the way to the venue, the music turned down low, so it sounded more like a hum.

My heart started racing when I saw us slow as we pulled into the venue. It wasn't long before we were sitting in our seats. We were close to the front which I was grateful for. I just wanted my eyes on her.

We sat and waited patiently for Laura to walk in. I watched Tyler fidgeting with his cufflinks while waiting for his bride to walk elegantly down the aisle. I saw the priest begin to get his notes out and stand at the podium as the heavy doors to the room opened slowly, a soft piano melody started echoing through the room as everyone stood waiting for the bride to appear.

I had a quick glance around the room. Some people were crying already, others had the biggest smiles on their faces. It was so lovely seeing the genuine expressions of people.

I focused my eyes on the open door, begging that she would be the first down the aisle, and just as I went to look at my watch for the time there she was.

My beautiful Freya.

Her beautiful smile lighting up the room as she started her slow walk towards Tyler. Her champagne gown clung to her curves, making me want her even more than I already did.

Her hair was in a messy side bun, a few strands of her glossy, auburn hair cascading down the side of her face.

I watched her eyes scan the room, searching for something.

Then I realised it was me.

Her grey eyes were searching for mine.

As soon as her eyes met mine, I saw her relax. Fuck, I missed her. I couldn't help my smile, it was the biggest I felt it had ever been.

I loved this woman.

Fuck, I was in bother.

CHAPTER TWENTY-FOUR

I was glad to be back with her. Okay we were only sitting at a table, but I was near her. We sat and enjoyed the speeches then our dinner which passed pleasantly. Once everything was finished, me and Freya sat and watched the events taking place in front of us, completely content with each other and what was going on around us. I placed my hand on her thigh, that spark alighting me once more.

"You look wonderful, Freya," I said as I leant into her ear, squeezing her leg slightly.

"As do you. I really dig you in a suit." She returned a compliment with a flirtatious tone. I loved flirty Freya.

"Oh, do you now? Maybe I will remember that for later," I teased her before winking at her. I moved my hand from her thigh and stood up. "I'm going to get a drink; would you like one?"

She nodded as she downed her white wine before putting her glass down. "Same again, please,"

I leant down and kissed her on her forehead, lingering

before walking towards the bar. Moments later I was back with a large glass of white wine as I placed it down in front of her. She took it and took a small sip. It seemed like she wanted to ask me something, but she didn't. Her eyes staring at her glass.

I didn't want to push it, but I felt like I wanted to ask her. I just sat down next to her as I pulled my phone out, feeling it vibrate in my pocket. I felt her eyes on me while I typed a quick response on my phone before answering her unanswered thoughts.

"Sorry," I said. "It's just work stuff, I need to head back tomorrow something has come up that I need to sort before New York on Monday." My voice deflated. I watched as she frowned at me, again biting her tongue to stop her from talking to me.

"You don't have to come with me, I can send James up on Sunday evening to get you if you would prefer?" I suggested. She took a few moments, and a few big mouthfuls of wine. This must have been her sixth glass, it was going to kick in sooner rather than later.

"I will come with you, I don't want to stay here without you," she said as she leant in to put a wine fuelled kiss on me. I could taste it on her breath, her lips were slightly wet, her breath warm and laced with wine. Shit wine, but never the less, I wanted more.

I cursed in my mind when the DJ interrupted our moment by calling Laura and Tyler onto the dance floor for their first dance. Freya immediately got up and made her way to the edge of the dance floor as Bruno Mars – Just the way you are started playing.

I smiled as I watched Tyler dance Laura all around the room. I couldn't help but softly move my hand slowly around her waist, then resting it on her stomach.

I pulled her into me and buried my head into her neck. My God she smelt divine. I couldn't get enough of her scent, perfume or no perfume she always smelt amazing.

"I really have missed you," I whispered against her ear. We didn't say anything, we just stood watching the newlyweds dancing as me and Freya stayed in our embrace. Just as the music was finishing, the DJ called the couples onto the dancefloor.

I laughed as Freya tried to get out of my grip. Oh no, this wasn't happening. She was going to dance with me.

I took her hand and pulled her gently towards the dance floor. She placed her arms around my neck, pulling me slightly closer to her. I rested my hands gently on the small of her back as I glided her effortlessly around the floor. She leant up towards me and gave me a soft kiss.

"Thank you for the last few days, it really has meant a lot," she said, her eyes glassy and giddy.

I leant down to her. "You're welcome. I've really enjoyed myself."

The evening seemed to whizz by. Freya only had a few

more wines and she was floored. She was mumbling and falling over. I shook my head at her, but also loved how care free she was. She tried to make a few moves on me subtly behind her mum and dads backs, which I was trying to hide from them. After half an hour of playing babysitter, Rose suggested we get her home.

"Are you okay getting her up to bed, Carter?" Rose asked, Harry's eyes on me.

"Yea, fine, I'll put her a bed then go to my own room." I smiled at Rose, then looked at Harry.

"Stay with her tonight, son, just in case she is unwell in the night." Harry nodded at me then disappeared into the kitchen.

"Go to bed, love, we will see you both in the morning. I'll put a glass of water on her bedside table." She smiled at me as she walked into the kitchen after Harry.

I still had Freya in my arms. I moved her over my shoulder and walked her upstairs, flopping onto her bed. I looked down at her as I tucked a loose bit of hair behind her ear. I could just stare at her, she is so stunning.

I fucking love her so hard, I couldn't wait to tell her. I started to undo my bowtie and shirt when Rose knocked quietly on the door.

"Only me, here's her water," she said passing me the glass. "She shouldn't be sick, but just keep an eye on her," her voice laced with concern. "Harry must really like you to let you stay in her room." She smiled at me.

"Thank him for me, Rose, I really appreciate it. Maybe it's the drink talking, but I just wanted to let you know how fond I am of your daughter. Not only fond, but so deeply in love with her. I will make her my wife one day, because I have never ever felt as strongly as I do with Freya," I said.

"I know, I can see how much you care for her, and she really does deserve it after everything she has been through. All I will say is, don't hurt her," she said forcefully.

"Understood." I nodded.

"Night, Carter," she said as she pulled the door to.

"Night, Rose," I replied back. I wasn't sure if she heard me.

I took my shirt off and folded it over Freya's chair in her room, then my trousers. I walked back over to her and rolled her slightly as I tugged on her zip before rolling her onto her back and pulling on her dress and sliding it down.

I marvelled at her glorious body. If only she was awake and conscious. A wicked thought crossed my mind, but I couldn't do it. Not to my angel.

I put one of my tee's over her head and lifted her into the bed. She made a few muffled noises before tucking her duvet under her face and returning to her peaceful, drunken slumber.

I slipped into bed next to her, nuzzling my face into her hair. It wasn't long before I joined her in a peaceful sleep.

"Ahhhh," I heard a groan coming from Freya next to

me. I wrapped my arm around her and pulled her close to me.

"Morning, sleepy head," I said quietly, still half asleep myself.

"Oh my God, my head," she moaned as she rolled over to face me. Her makeup was smudged all round her face, but she still looked beautiful.

"Why do I feel so rough?" she whined at me, burying her head in my chest.

"That would have something to do with the amount of wine you drank, angel." I tried not to make it sound like I wanted to burst into laughter.

"Why didn't you stop me?" she said, pulling her head up and throwing me an icy glare.

"Oh, so this is my fault?" I chuckled quietly.

"Yes," she snapped.

"Oh, ain't you a little bear with a sore head." I laughed again. She pouted at me and then crinkled her nose. "But you are a cute, beautiful, sexy, irresistible bear with a sore head," I cooed before tilting her lips up towards me as I leant down and kissed her softly. I wanted to do more but I had to get a move on.

"I don't want to leave, wish we could stay here one last night, but as usual work gets in the way." I sighed.

"I don't want to leave either, but it will only be one day and then we are going New York," she said with a smile creeping on her face.

"That's right, baby," I said kissing her again. "I'm going to get ready, I'll meet you downstairs," I whispered as I left the cosy, warm bed and made my way to my bedroom at the end of the hallway.

After a quick shower I went downstairs, dumping my duffle bag by the front door. Freya's suitcase was sitting next to mine. I didn't want to intrude on their goodbyes.

"Don't leave it to long next time, my darling," Rose said as she took her into a tight embrace.

I got emotional watching her and her dad's goodbye. They had such a strong bond. Her mum then came over to me and took me into a loving embrace.

I headed to the car and loaded the bags into the boot while rose and Freya were still talking and having one last hug, her dad standing proudly in the doorway.

"You ready?" I asked before closing the boot down and she nodded at me. I watched her walk slowly to the car, I opened my door, sliding in as Freya went to open hers when we heard a voice.

I froze, the hairs on the back of my neck standing up.

I knew that voice, and so did she.

I climbed back out the car and stood on the spot next to her, I quickly took her hand into mine, squeezing it letting her know I was with her and not letting her go. I didn't know what this prick wanted but I knew deep down what it was. He must know. Aimee must have told him. Fuck. My heart was beating in my chest, I could hear the blood pumping in my ears. I had never been so scared in my life.

"What do you want, Jake?" Freya said harshly. "First outside Laura's house, and now here." I turned to face her. what the fuck did she mean 'first outside Laura's house?' Why didn't she tell me? I was even more annoyed now.

I tightened my grip as I saw him walk towards us.

"I need to speak to you, please, Freya. Give me five minutes." I watched her turn towards her mum and dad, as if she were waiting for them to tell her what to do, but they just stood there looking as confused as her.

I should have dragged her away, put her straight in the car and drove away without looking back. But my feet felt like they were glued to the floor. Jake took a step closer to us.

"Don't go!" he called out, and I felt Freya's grip loosen. I watched her brow furrow as she looked at him confused.

"Please don't go," he pleaded. "I fucked up, Freya, I don't want to lose you again. Especially to him," he hissed as he faced me with a death stare. I tried to swallow but I felt like my throat was closing up. I felt like I couldn't breathe.

"You won't have a chance to lose me again. I've moved on, so have you. Where is she anyway? Your doting fiancé," she snarled at him, she was livid.

I loved angry Freya, as long as it wasn't me she was angry at and the way this was going, she was going to be angry with me in about five minutes if this is what I think he is going to expose.

"It's over, Freya, I called it off," he said quietly. I watched as he looked to the ground and up at Freya. Her mouth dropped open at his confession. She dropped my hand and moved towards Jake. I wanted to scream and shout and pull her back towards me, but I couldn't. Fear was coursing through me and I didn't know what to do.

She looked back at me as she stood in front of Jake, before she focused back on him.

"What do you mean you called it off?" she asked inquisitively. He laughed at her question as if it was the most stupid thing to ask in the world.

"Has your new lover boy not told you?"

I watched his face twist as he started to tell her, tell her my secret that I wasn't ready to share. I tried to step forward, but I couldn't. My heart broke right there, and there was nothing I could do. I couldn't work out if it was confusion on her face or heartbreak.

"Let me fill you in," he said bringing her attention back to him. "When I bumped into him the night before last when he was leaving the pub, Aimee changed, she said she knew him, he was an ex..." he over exaggerated the 'ex'.

My heart stopped, I am sure of it. My mouth dry, my throat swelling again. She looked at me again, I couldn't bring myself to look into her beautiful grey eyes. I was staring straight through her.

"Yeah, she told me they had an arrangement, she was one of his *flavours*." Jake was clearly getting wound up at this point. I couldn't see her face, I couldn't see what she was thinking, and it was making me panic even more.

Then, just like that she turned around to face me. The blood flushed to her face, her eyes bulging out as they rimmed with unshed tears. I am sure I could hear her heart breaking in front of me. And like an idiot I just stood there, again. Not moving from the spot.

"Is this true?" she asked. I wanted to reply but I couldn't, my tongue tied.

"IS THIS TRUE?" she screamed at me.

I dropped my head in defeat, I couldn't deny it. I couldn't lie to her. I had been lying this whole time, how could I continue now?

"Yes," I said, heartbroken, embarrassed, ashamed, a liar.

Jake continued to explain to her my dirty revenge plan not leaving anything out of his explanation. I just stared at my feet, I became a coward when I needed to scream from my lungs that I loved her, that I regret everything and did from the moment I first laid eyes on her.

"You just wanted revenge?" she snarled at me.

Tears now freely flowing down her beautiful face, the beautiful face I have spent every minute getting to know every single feature on it. I moved a step forward towards her.

"Don't!" she shouted at me, warning me.

"Freya, please let me explain..." I begged, she shook her head, still not looking at me. I had to tell her. "Yes, at first. That was my plan." I winced. "You were just going to be a revenge fuck, but I fell for you. I fell for you the moment I laid eyes on you in Jools' office." I dropped my shoulders, I felt broken.

Everything suddenly felt heavy, like a huge weight had now been burdened on my shoulders. I didn't even know if she was listening, but I carried on. "I should have told you, but how could I explain that without sounding like a complete arsehole?"

My eyes brimming, trying to keep it together in front of her. I heard him snigger from behind Freya, I just wanted to run at him and destroy him. I was so angry, but heartbreak consumed me. I took this moment to move closer to her, she didn't move. We stood so close, but I had never felt further away from her.

"Please, Freya, come home," I begged her, the tears flowing from her glistening grey eyes.

I wish they were glistening out of happiness and not complete betrayal and heartache. My blood started boiling when Jake wrapped his arms around her shoulders.

She was mine.

How fucking dare he.

I had to walk away. If I didn't I would smash Jake's face into the floor and I wouldn't stop until he was bleeding out beneath my touch. I stepped back towards my car, the bumper hitting the back of my legs.

"Baby," I said in a last attempt. "I love you…" I trailed off, knowing this was the first time I had said it to her, even though I wanted to tell her a lot sooner than this moment here. This wasn't the way it was supposed to go.

I could feel her parents' eyes on me. I had never felt so ashamed in all my life. Normally shit like this wouldn't bother me, I would be bragging about it, shrugging it off like no fucks given. But it was different this time. It was her. My love.

I watched as she shook Jake off of her, moving a step closer to me again, but no words left her lips. Just her eyes on mine, I felt her slipping from me. Slipping from my grip.

"I've got to go, Freya. Please come with me," I begged. She didn't move, didn't say anything. I lifted her suitcase out of my boot and walked slowly over to her parents' pathway, placing it there gently. I didn't look up, I couldn't bear to face them. I stood in front of Freya, her eyes on the floor, her face tear stained from the tears from me.

I expected her to move, but she didn't. I knew she loved me, I knew she didn't want to stay but she wouldn't come with me. Pride wouldn't allow her.

I kissed her forehead gently, taking in her scent as I did. I had to, I needed to remember how she smelt. I didn't know when I would next see her again, or if I would ever see her again.

"You know where I am. You have the flight and hotel details. Please, baby, I don't want to lose you," I said quietly as I stepped away from her for what felt like the last time.

I slid into my car and turned the engine on. Before pulling away I looked into the rear-view mirror, my eyes finding her.

I hope she knows it is killing me to leave.

I finally pulled my eyes from her and pulled away my heart breaking into my chest. Shattering into a thousand pieces. The blackness taking over once more.

They say the harder you love, the harder you fall right?

Well, I felt like I was crashing.

And in that moment, I had done what I originally planned. I had broken her.

Completely obliterated her heart, and there was nothing I could do to change it.

ACKNOWLEDGEMENTS

To my followers, thank you for the continued support as always for reading and sharing my books and constant love i feel from you all.

Irish Ink:

Wonderful Leigh. You have been amazing, I really don't know what I would have done without you. Not only have you made my book look amazing when all it looked like was a big essay, you have made the book what it is with the wonderful cover. I am honestly so grateful for all of your help.

Lindsey & Nikki, thank you so much for everything these past few months. I am so grateful for all your help through this journey. I feel like we have formed a wonderful friendship, so thank you.

If you enjoyed this book, please leave a review on Amazon & Goodreads.

Printed in Great Britain
by Amazon